IF SHE FAVOURS YOU

HARLEY ROSE

Text copyright © Harley Rose 2019

All Rights Reserved.

This book is a work of fiction. Any references to historical events, real people, or real places are used fictitiously. Names, characters, and places are products of the author's imagination.

Front cover image by Gale Ryan.

First published by Gleeful Publishing in 2019.

Quotations taken from

Charles Dickens' *Great Expectations* and *A Tale of Two Cities*,

Edgar Allan Poe's *Annabel Lee*,

William Shakespeare's *Othello*.

ISBN: 978-1-9162372-0-9

To my family, who showed me what love is.

'Love her, love her, love her! If she favours you, love her. If she wounds you, love her. If she tears your heart to pieces - and as it gets older and stronger, it will tear deeper - love her, love her, love her'

-CHARLES DICKENS, *Great Expectations*

Chapter 1

I was eighteen years old when I realised I was predictable.

I was sitting in Vellichor, a second-hand bookshop that doubled as a café, for the third time in three days. My boyfriend was talking to me. As usual, I was too distracted by the books behind him to listen; there had been an influx of new donations, all with pristine covers.

When his voice started to get louder, I tried to tune back into the conversation. Within seconds, however, my gaze drifted to a strand of bleached blond hair that was resting over one of his eyes. I reached out to tuck it behind his ear and he grunted loudly.

'Emily, can you please listen for once?' He slammed his hand down onto the table and I drew back.

'Sorry.' I looked down at the tie-dyed pumps on my feet. I couldn't remember the last time I'd worn a different pair of shoes; even my footwear was predictable.

James rubbed the back of his neck and didn't return my sheepish grin. As he began to speak again, I saw Vellichor's sole employee amble towards us.

'Hi Mr Costas,' I said, placing our used utensils on his tray. 'That was as lovely as ever.'

Mr Costas was around fifty, the same age as my parents, and had moved to England from Greece when he was twenty. I'd always wondered why the tiny middle-of-nowhere town of Kellerwick appealed to him more than the sixty or so beaches of Skiathos.

He beamed at me, his crooked front teeth on full display. 'Thank you, Miss Emily.'

'God, you could at least let me finish,' James said. I turned back to him, just as he ran his fingers through his hair. It rested over his eye once again.

Mr Costas cleared his throat. 'Would my favourite couple like any more food before I close?' he asked, gesturing at the empty tables around us. 'I am free to make whatever you'd like.'

'We're fine,' said James, sitting back in his chair. I nodded as Mr Costas left again. He frowned at James as he did so.

'What were you saying?' I asked, leaning forward. I tried to ignore the reddish tint that was appearing on James' cheeks and how it perfectly matched the scratchy rose carpet.

'I want to break up, Emily.'

My eyes met his. 'You what?'

'I want to break up with you,' he repeated, more softly that time. 'I think we should start this summer with a clean break.'

'So, you want to split up? Just like that?' I could hear my voice trembling as I spoke, and I tried to focus on that. Focus on that and on the way my hands were shaking rather than what James was saying. I inhaled as deeply as I could, wondering if I could have misheard him. Twice. Or if, maybe, he was just joking because he wanted to get my attention; we had no reason to split up.

'Emily, I've thought this through. We're not right for each other anymore. We're too different.'

As he carried on listing excuses, I looked down at his hands again. They weren't shaking like mine. He had wrapped them around his mug so tightly that his fingers were growing pale. It seemed as if he had taken the task of making my life less predictable into his own hands.

'What am I supposed to do in September?' I asked, weighing up the likelihood of the whole situation being a bad dream. Suddenly, I couldn't feel the cushioned seat of the chair beneath me, and I could sense my eyes wanting to drift shut. I forced them open. 'We'll be living in the same accommodation and doing the same art course; I can't exactly avoid you.'

James' grip loosened on his coffee cup and his eyes flickered downwards. 'I'm not going with you to uni.'

'What?' My voice didn't even sound like mine at that point; it was too high pitched; too desperate. I tried to ground myself, focusing on how the smell of James' aftershave suffocated the musk of paperbacks and coffee. I almost heaved after a large gulp of breath and knew I wasn't dreaming.

'I'm taking a gap year.'

'Since when?' He didn't reply. I swallowed and tried again. 'Since when did you have plans other than university?' As James opened his mouth, his phone lit up with a notification. I looked down at the table, just as he covered the screen with his hand. 'Is there someone else?'

He sighed. 'I've made up my –'

I didn't wait for him to carry on talking; instead, I picked up my bag and left. I waved half-heartedly at Mr Costas as I did so, whilst expertly moving between the myriad of tables and chairs.

My house was only a few minutes' walk away, but James' was on the street before mine, so I opted for the longer route home. Taking advantage of the silent summer evening, I let my mind replay the conversation. Then again. Then once more.

I barely paid attention to the neighbours I passed, them being more familiar with my mother than with me, and as I reached my house, I felt tears starting to well up in my eyes. I blinked them away furiously; I was Emily Davis, and I wasn't going to cry over a boy. Even if that boy was my first boyfriend and the only friend I'd made in school. Even if he was beautiful and talented and -

'Emily!' My thought process was interrupted by my dad shouting to me from the front door. With his wide shoulders and six-foot figure, he filled the frame almost completely. 'Hello, mo stoirín.' Much like Mr Costas, he'd lived in England for thirty years, but had never lost his unmistakable Irish accent, or his habit of slipping into Gaelic. I made myself smile as I trudged up the drive. 'Good to see you're back before curfew.' He winked before turning around and walking into the kitchen. I'd never had a curfew in my life and we both knew it.

I sniffed discreetly before following him inside and seeing my mum. She was standing in front of the island, placing various food stuffs into a wicker basket, and my dad was now next to her. He still had his suit on, even though he'd returned home from his law firm before I'd left. He hadn't even loosened his tie.

Next to him, my mum looked tiny; her short brunette hair was tied into the world's smallest ponytail and her head barely reached his chin. Even though I hadn't inherited her delicate facial features, it wasn't hard to see that I'd got my height from her. I started to wonder if James had thought I wasn't pretty enough for him; maybe he wouldn't have dumped me if I'd had my mum's small, snub nose or her enviable waist.

'How was your James?' my dad asked, snapping my thoughts away from ifs and maybes. I blinked rapidly as he tried to squeeze a muffin into the basket and Mum batted his hands away.

'Yes, how was he?' She looked up for the first time since I'd walked in. She was wearing a novelty apron, like she always did in the kitchen, regardless of whether she was cooking or not; I'd probably also inherited my predictable-ness from her. That particular apron was pink, and adorned with a caricature of Elton John, as well as the words '*Don't Go Baking My Tart*'. I felt my stomach tighten, and not because of how out of place the pun looked on a woman who hardly smiled.

'He was alright.' I walked over to one of our cupboards and took a glass out. 'He broke up with me, though.' I marvelled at the way my voice barely wavered that time.

'He broke up with you?' my mum asked as I took the water filter from the fridge. 'Are you alright?'

I resisted the urge to reply with a sarcastic *of course I'm alright; why wouldn't I be? I've only been dumped for no reason*; the truth was, I didn't feel as bad as I had in Vellichor. In all honesty, I was just more surprised than upset. I guessed that it could be the shock, and that the next day I could wake up feeling hysterical and desperate for James to date me again. Then again, I thought, I was probably just surprised that something out of the ordinary had happened.

'Yeah, I'm fine.' I poured myself a drink. My hands were still shaking slightly, but not enough to spill any water.

'Are you sure, sweetheart?' As my dad spoke, his eyebrows furrowed together. I sat on a stool opposite him, listening as he gently tapped his foot on the floor.

'I'm very sure,' I replied. 'He was never my –' I paused. 'Mo chroi anyway.'

My dad's expression softened at my hesitant use of the Gaelic term, but my mum spoke before he could help correct my flawed pronunciation.

'Oh my goodness, these cakes have gluten in.' She peered at the empty plastic packet in front of her. 'Oh dear, what if they're allergic?'

Without any instruction from me, a sigh escaped my lips. It didn't matter what conversation you were having with my mum; if she suddenly thought of something, you could bet any money that you'd spend the next fifteen to fifty minutes discussing that instead. As much as I wanted to wallow in what had just happened, I decided to humour her; that felt like a better idea than getting emotional about something I couldn't change.

'What if who's allergic?'

'Linda and Alana Wilson.'

'The new neighbours,' said my dad at the same time. 'We were just helping them move the last of their stuff in, and your mum took a shine to them. She has now decided, therefore, to try and make them feel welcome. With a basket.'

'They won't feel welcome if I make them ill. Judging from what Linda said, that poor family has been through enough.'

There was a sudden silence in the room. I looked between my parents, but neither made any attempt to speak. My initial assumption that my mother was exaggerating, as she was prone to do, was replaced with an uneasy feeling that something legitimately serious was being discussed.

I tried to lighten the mood, not even considering the irony of the newly dumped person having to be the one to do that. 'Why, because they've moved next door to us? We're not that bad.' My dad laughed slightly, but then shook his head. 'What's happened to them?'

My mum clicked her tongue as she started to pick out the offending cakes, replacing them with satsumas. 'It's Alana. She's Linda's daughter and she's your age. She's ill.'

From the tone of my mum's voice, I could guess that Alana didn't have a case of the summer flu.

'What, is she dying?' I could also guess that I had maybe read *The Fault in our Stars* a few too many times. I sighed again, this time at myself for starting to think about a love story.

'No!' My parents' quick response should have relaxed me, but something about their sense of urgency unsettled my stomach further.

'So, what's wrong with her?'

'When she was younger, she had bacterial meningitis.' My mum paused and looked at my dad. 'I think. That's what Linda said, isn't it?' He nodded at her. 'She got really sick, though it's gone now.'

'Then why is she still not well?'

'She's still suffering the after-effects and –' my mum cut herself off. I watched my dad sidle back towards her. 'And Emily, you've had an eventful evening; you need some sleep.'

'You're just not going to tell me? I'll be doing nothing this summer except for sitting in my room, Mum. You might as well let me know who'll be sitting in the room opposite; she'll be less than a metre away.'

At those words, my mum's eyes widened a little.

'Of course! You'll be free this summer now,' she said, adding a jar of jam to the basket. I tried not to think about how carelessly she recited that observation. 'You can spend time with Alana! Linda gave the impression that she hasn't got many friends.'

My dad raised his eyebrows at me.

'But Mum, I don't know her,' I argued, my gaze flickering over to the freezer. As much as I pitied Alana, all I really wanted to do for the foreseeable future was bury myself in tubs of Ben and Jerry's. I told you I was predictable. 'Plus, I'm moving away at the end of summer.'

'Emily, please. It might make you feel better if you try and be friends with her.'

My dad was still looking at me, his teeth gnawing at his bottom lip. I nodded.

'Fine.' I stood up and walked over to the stairs with my water. 'I'll try. But first, I want to sleep.'

'Night, stoirín.'

'Goodnight, Emily.'

I could hear them talking to each other as I walked upstairs; if my house was quiet, kitchen conversations could be heard from any room. I didn't focus on their words, though, and instead straightened the canvases that were hanging on the wall.

As I stepped inside my room and dropped my bag, I noticed immediately that the light was on in the bedroom next door. All I could see, however, was a bed and a load of boxes. That was, until a girl stepped into my eyeline. I walked over to the desk below my window, reasoning that she must be Alana.

She looked directly at me, and I saw she had long, curly hair that was almost the same shade of red-orange as the wall behind me. She was wearing ripped jeans with a faded t-shirt. Considering she'd spent a summer day moving to a new house, she looked beautiful: far too beautiful to be friends with someone as plain as me.

I squinted, trying to decipher the writing on her shirt. Even though I wanted to wave at her, or to smile at least, I couldn't pull my gaze away from her chest. Then, all of a sudden, she was replaced with familiar black material. The old neighbours had left their curtains.

Groaning, I looked down at my arms and cursed them for staying by my sides. As I did so, my eyes latched onto a framed picture of James and me. I felt my shoulders slump as I thought back to our conversation, and my mum's reaction when I told her about it, and I searched for a distraction before my hands could start shaking again.

I looked over to my bed and the paint-covered sheet beside it. Within seconds, I'd grabbed a blank canvas and a pencil. I knelt on the floor. Though I knew that a few seconds hadn't been long enough to look at her properly, I started a rough sketch of Alana's face. It had been months since I'd drawn someone for the first time, but my pencil flew across the page with little instruction from me. I tried not to think about James, or about how weird Alana would assume I was if she ever found out what I was doing.

When the outline of her hair and face was done, I returned to the window. Before I began to pull my blind down, however, I saw Alana again. She was peeking through the gap in the middle of her curtains and looking down. I wondered if I'd gotten her parting right in my drawing; I'd sketched a middle one, but it seemed to be more to the side. As I studied her hairline, she looked up. We made eye contact again, but this time was different; her eyes were red, and tears were rolling down her cheeks. Before I could acknowledge her, she'd turned away. A few seconds later, her light went out, leaving the tiny section of room that I could see in darkness.

Chapter 2

The next morning, I was woken up by a knock on the front door. As I heard my parents greet someone, I rubbed open my eyes and reached for my phone.

I was halfway through drafting a *good morning* text to James when I remembered. My thumbs danced over the keyboard before I dropped the phone onto my pillow. I wondered if he'd done the same thing, then thought back to how he'd hidden his messages from me in Vellichor. I sighed to myself, though I still didn't feel as sad as I thought I should. A little empty, perhaps. Just not sad. Not even as sad as I had done the day before.

Hearing my muscles give a satisfying click, I stretched my arms above my head and swung my legs onto the carpet. I walked over to my window. As I opened my blind, I saw that next door's curtains were already drawn. I then remembered just what I'd seen before I went to bed. Alana had looked as if she'd been crying for a long time, and the sudden change in her appearance had been alarming. I wondered what could have upset her enough to warrant that reaction; it could be her illness, or maybe the move, or something else entirely. My reaction to James breaking up with me seemed pathetic in comparison.

I was looking to see if Alana was inside her room, when I heard a creaking noise from behind me. I turned to see my mum wrinkling her nose in my doorway.

'I don't know how you can stand looking at that bright yellow first thing in the morning,' she said, gesturing towards the wall I was standing in front of.

During the previous summer, my dad and I had decided to paint each section of my room a different colour. Aside from the mint green ceiling, my mum had disapproved completely, and she took every opportunity to remind me of that. I bit back a smile.

'Good morning to you too, Mum.' She frowned at my false gaiety. 'Yes, I'm having a lovely morning as a singleton. No, I can't believe it's been ten months since I've been one either.'

She tutted. 'Emily, we have a guest downstairs. You should get dressed.'

'A guest?'

She nodded and turned away. 'Join us when you're ready.'

I glanced back to my window, before I hurried to my wardrobe and scanned the colour-coordinated outfits. My mother hadn't specified to dress smartly, so I reached for my favourite harem trousers. They were black, with splashes of colour on the ankles, and I grabbed a white vest top too.

I heard laughter as I walked into the living room, then I saw my mum sitting on our sofa with a cup of tea in her hand, and one leg crossed over the other. A woman sat beside her. She had greying, shoulder-length ginger hair, thick rimmed glasses and a black pant suit. Her legs were slightly splayed to the sides and her head was tilted back.

'You must be Emmy!' the woman said as she looked over to me. She jumped to her feet then pulled me in for a hug. I held back a splutter as her arms wrapped around me and I looked up at her. She seemed to be even taller than my dad.

'I'm Emily, yes,' I said half-breathlessly when she let me go. I looked between her and my mum as I took a step back.

'This is Mrs Wilson,' my mum said. 'Our new neighbour.'

I looked back at the woman. 'Oh! Nice to meet you.'

She grinned at me. 'And it's wonderful to meet you. My Al said you saw her last night.'

'You saw Alana?' My dad appeared in the doorway adjusting his tie. 'Before you got back?' I wondered if he'd cut himself whilst shaving; there was a little piece of tissue stuck to his cheek.

'No. Just at my window before I slept.' I watched as he began patting down the pockets on his suit.

'Yes, and I'm glad you have a view of each other,' Mrs Wilson said, taking my hand and sitting back down on the sofa. I sat between her and my mum. 'Your parents have told me a lot about you, and I think you two could be great friends.'

'They really could.' My mum stood up and retrieved a set of keys from the table. She walked over to my dad and pressed them into his hands, before slowly peeling the tissue off his face. He kissed the top of her forehead and she smiled. I almost did the same; it was rare to see my mum show affection, and I lived through the snippets of love I saw in her caring for my dad. 'Linda, would you like more tea?'

'No thanks, chuck.' Mrs Wilson lifted her half-full mug and took a swig before setting it back down.

I watched my dad leave for work, calling *goodbye* as he did so. A second later, my mum retreated into the kitchen. I wondered if I should tell Mrs Wilson about how upset her daughter had seemed. Aware that Alana might not want me to, however, I reached for one of the biscuits my mum had set out. As I nibbled, Mrs Wilson spoke again.

'Your parents said they didn't tell you what's happening to Alana. Is that right?' I nodded, and her cheery expression drooped slightly. 'I suppose there's no point wasting words. To cut a long story short, Emmy, she's suffering from sensorineural hearing loss. She's going deaf.'

I tried to swallow the bit of bourbon in my mouth so I could respond, but I just felt a chocolatey paste coat my tongue. I had no idea what I'd expected to hear about Alana, but I knew it wasn't that. Suddenly, her distraught appearance made sense.

'I'm sorry,' I mumbled, hoping no crumbs escaped.

'It's not your fault, love.' Her voice was suddenly quiet. She gulped down the rest of her tea. 'I was coming to thank your parents for the basket they dropped off last night, when we got to talking about you. I really would like you to meet my Al.'

'You would?' My voice was strangely wheezy, as if Mrs Wilson had hugged me again.

She nodded. 'Alana drifted away from her friends before we moved, and she acts like she doesn't care, but–' Linda paused as she stood and brushed herself down. 'But I would like her to meet you, especially after what happened with your boyfriend.'

I silently cursed my mum for telling Linda about James; her daughter was losing her hearing, so me losing my boyfriend was a lot less significant.

'Then I'll gladly meet her,' I said. I stood too, ignoring the fact that I had less social skills than a skunk and had never met a deaf person before. 'When were you thinking?'

'This afternoon? I have a job interview at one and I hate the thought of leaving Al alone in a new house.'

'That's fine,' I said, my stomach fluttering only slightly at the thought of meeting another stranger that day. I wouldn't have predicted myself ever feeling that okay about the prospect. 'I look forward to it.'

Linda pulled me in for another hug, her smile having returned. Before she did so, I noticed she had chartreuse eyes, as well as a light smattering of freckles on her neck and face. I wondered if Alana did too.

'I'll tell her to expect you, Emmy,' she said before stepping into the hallway. 'Sarah, hon? I'm heading out.'

My mum bustled over, having tied one of her aprons around herself. It had been an anniversary present from my dad, and was decorated with a cartoon picture of a chef making pizza, as well as the words '*I adough you.*'

'Thank you for coming over, Linda,' she said. I tried not to laugh at her attempt to kiss Mrs Wilson's cheek, or at how small she looked beside her.

'My pleasure, chuck!'

'I'm proud of you,' Mum said when Mrs Wilson had left. 'See! Being dumped doesn't mean you have to have a lonely summer.'

'I guess not.' Sometimes I wondered how my mum had ever got her job as a teacher in a primary school; sure, she was only part-time, but she really lacked the empathy to be around kids all day.

'Now, come and get some breakfast,' she said, walking back into the kitchen. 'You need to be ready to make a good first impression.'

Chapter 3

Before I even raised my fist to knock at the Wilsons' door, Linda opened it and greeted me.

'Thanks for coming, Emmy.' She stepped out of the house and gestured for me to go in. 'I'm running a bit late, so I'll see you later. Al's ready for you!' With that, she took a bobble off her wrist and ran down the drive, pulling her hair into a ponytail.

I debated shouting *good luck*, but realised she was probably too far away to hear me. Instead, I stepped inside the hall and closed the front door.

'You're Emmy Davis?' I looked up to see Alana standing at the top of the staircase. Her hair was straight, falling in a silky sheet around her shoulders, and she was wearing black skinny jeans that she filled beautifully. She also wore a cherry-red crop top. Although her stomach wasn't flat, she was thinner than me: a perfect size, and I had to fight to draw my eyes away from her glistening navel piercing.

She started to walk down the stairs and I dug my nails into my palm, trying to prompt myself to answer. I didn't know if I was supposed to speak loudly, or if I should emphasise my lip movements. As Mrs Wilson hadn't mentioned it, I avoided doing either.

'Emily, yes. Your mum just –' Alana reached the bottom of the staircase and stood in front of me, her arms crossed. She wasn't as tall as her mum, but I still had to tilt my head up to look at her. Once again. I wondered whether I should mention how upset she'd seemed the night before. Once again, I decided against it; I didn't want to make her uncomfortable. 'She just calls me Emmy.'

Alana's eyes were green like Mrs Wilson's, but darker and framed with thicker eyelashes. Her freckles were more prominent too. I wondered if I should have enunciated more clearly, or if I needed to repeat myself, when she replied.

'Makes sense; she has a thing for nicknames.' With that, Alana spun on her heel and began to walk down the hall. Despite the fluffy pink socks she wore, she looked more elegant than anyone I'd ever met. I hurried after her, skirting around the boxes littering the floor. 'My mum told me you and your boyfriend broke up,' she continued, as I followed her into the kitchen. It looked just like an emptier version of mine; they had even put their calendar on the same wall as us. 'I'm sorry.' She placed two bowls onto the island.

'It's not your fault,' I replied after a few seconds, wondering why I was preoccupied with watching Alana walk over to her freezer instead of thinking back to James.

'What was his name?' she asked, pulling out a large cream-coloured tub.

'James.' I watched her scoop ice cream into the bowls and then take out a jar of pick 'n' mix sweets from a cupboard beside her. 'James Fernsby.'

Alana hummed in response before sprinkling a handful of sweets into each bowl and returning the tub to the freezer. She motioned for me to pick up one of the dishes and follow her into the living room.

'The best thing to do after a break-up is eat junk food and watch crappy films,' she told me, sitting on the couch in front of the television. It was grey and covered in bright cushions, each a different colour. I loved it; my mum would have hated it. I wondered if she'd seen it the day before. Alana curled her legs up underneath her, then patted the space beside her until I sat down too. 'Though, this is me assuming you're not vegan.' Alana looked from my face to the bowl in my hand. 'You're not, are you?'

I shook my head. 'No, but I could be lactose-intolerant.' My words tumbled out before I could think about them or consider why I was joking around with someone I didn't even know. When Alana smiled, however, I was beyond glad that I hadn't overthought my word choice.

'Then join the club,' she said, before scooping a spoonful of ice cream into her mouth. I could see that she was still smiling as she ate.

'Wait, you can't eat dairy?'

Alana swallowed and removed the spoon, drawing my attention to a dimple that had appeared on her cheek. 'I can, because I just did.'

I opened my mouth but couldn't come up with a retort. Alana chuckled, and I was caught off guard by the sound; it was light, airy. Compelling.

'I'm not lactose-intolerant, by the way,' I said finally, still staring at her smile.

Alana picked up the remote beside her. 'Me neither.' She turned the television on and I felt myself smiling too as I started to eat.

The combination of jelly sweets and dairy was almost heavenly; it felt like something Willy Wonka would have endorsed and I ate quite happily as I watched Alana scroll through a list of films. Eventually, she decided on one I'd never heard of and she switched the subtitles on as it began to play. Less than a minute later, she looked at me, her brow slightly creased.

'I'm sorry, do you mind me having the captions on?' she asked. 'I know some people hate them.'

'I don't mind at all.'

The film was good, or at least as good as a cheesy rom-com can be when watched the day after a break-up. It was about a teenage girl whose father told her she was too young to date anybody. I was genuinely quite invested in the plot when Alana paused the film and turned to me with a groan, tucking her hair behind her ear and revealing a pale blue hearing aid. I averted my eyes as quickly as I could, in case she thought I was staring.

'Why do adults think teenagers are too young to fall in love?' she asked, gently tapping the remote against her leg. 'We aren't too young to be upset, or to be angry, so why do parents say we're too young to love someone?'

I cocked my head to the side. 'Well, my parents have been together since they met in university, so they would never tell me that.'

Alana looked at me for a minute before continuing. 'That's really cute, but seriously. This guy –' She gestured wildly at the TV. 'This guy thinks he knows more about his daughter's feelings than she does. How is that possible?'

'Maybe he's just trying to look out for her,' I suggested, captivated by how Alana's eyes grew wider as the conversation went on. Their brightness was enchanting, and my own hazel eyes felt dull in comparison. 'He could be trying to stop her from getting hurt.' I realised as I spoke that I wanted Alana to disagree with me; I wanted her to convince me of her point of view, just because that would mean talking to her for a little while longer with no distraction.

'Or maybe he thinks you can't truly experience love until you get to some arbitrary age that teenagers can't even consider reaching.' I felt the corner of my mouth twitch. 'Come on, you must have a strong opinion about this! You're eighteen but were in love with James, right?'

I shifted on the couch and placed my empty bowl on the floor, immediately missing the smell of vanilla.

'I don't know if I was in love exactly,' I began. 'If I was, I think I'd have been more upset about us breaking up. Like, I'm sad, but I'm not going to stop all my clocks and wear the same outfit for the rest of my life.'

Alana laughed a little, and I felt a warm sensation in my stomach. 'Good. Davis is a much better surname than Havisham.'

'Do you like Charles Dickens?' I asked instinctively, surprised that she'd acknowledged my reference. 'His books are my favourites.'

'I like *Great Expectations*,' Alana said, pointing to a box beside the TV that was labelled *BOOKS*. She continued, faster that time, 'I actually have two copies of it; one for highlighting and writing notes, and one in mint condition.' As Alana met my eyes again, she bit her lip and looked down. 'Wow, that makes me sound like a nerd.'

'No, no,' I said, as she twirled a strand of hair around her finger. 'Any novel that's worth reading provokes enough thoughts to fill its margins.' Alana narrowed her eyes at me, as if she was trying to gage my sincerity. 'And you know, I've never met anybody else my age who actually likes old books.'

She dropped her hair again, a smirk threatening to emerge on her face. 'Yeah, but from what my mum said, you don't get out a lot, so you probably haven't met many people.'

'How very rude!' Without thinking, I picked up a mauve cushion that was beside me and gently hit Alana's shoulder with it. I thought back to how awestruck I'd been in front of her just an hour ago, and our conversation suddenly felt too good; too relaxed; too not-awkward-at-all to be happening.

Alana laughed and took the cushion off me before hugging it to her chest. 'So, as you never really had it with James, do you think you want to experience what love feels like?'

I mentally scolded myself for jinxing the comfort of the situation.

'I'm not sure,' I said, wishing my own hair was long enough to fiddle with as I brought my hands together. 'I mean, part of me has always wanted what my parents have, but part of me is terrified at the thought of liking someone that much. Do you know what I mean?'

'Do I know about being scared to love someone?' Alana turned away again and pressed play on the remote. 'You could say that.'

I wracked my brain, but I couldn't find the words to ask her what she meant. Instead, I simply watched out of the corner of my eye as Alana kept hold of the cushion and stared at the TV. When the credits eventually started to roll, I felt my heart begin to beat faster.

'Have you ever been in love?' I heard myself ask. After a second, I realised I didn't want to hear her answer; I didn't want to be told she had a boyfriend back where she'd moved from, and I hated the idea of her having been fearful of loving someone. I couldn't justify either thought.

'Oh, darling,' she began dramatically, tossing her hair behind her back with a quick hand movement. 'I'm the type of girl who's always falling in love. Sometimes that's the best way to be.'

'Only sometimes?'

'Only sometimes.' Before I could question her further, a message tone and vibrating noise rang out. Alana retrieved a phone from her pocket. I watched silently until she looked up again. 'My mum got the job,' she said eventually, smiling slightly. 'And she's having her first shift now. Despite the fact she's wearing a pant suit.' Alana giggled as she typed a reply. 'And she wants to know if I've made you fluent in BSL yet.'

'BSL?'

'British Sign Language.' I really should have guessed that. 'I know she told you I'm hard of hearing, and I find it easier than reading lips. Though, my hearing aids do a great job of helping me follow conversations.'

'Well, I already know the BSL alphabet,' I said, thinking back to the assembly on Deaf culture we'd had in school. We'd each been given bright yellow notecards afterwards, on which cartoon hands demonstrated how to fingerspell. 'But I'd like to learn more.'

I tried to hide it, but I loved the idea of Alana teaching me how to speak to her. I was reminded of being in primary school, and of those rare occasions when I was invited to play with the popular girls; I felt the same sense of pride, but this time far more intensely.

'In that case, maybe you should learn something more exciting.'

'I don't know what you mean.'

'Bullshit,' Alana replied, signing it at the same time.

I tried not to laugh. 'Excuse me?'

Alana repeated herself, her gestures consisting of violently pretending to drop something out of her hands.

'Bullshit. It's one of my favourite signs.' I couldn't help but let my mouth fall open slightly; that wasn't the first word I'd expected to learn. 'Come on, the best part of learning a new language is learning how to swear in it!'

I closed my mouth again and gulped. Though I wasn't about to admit it to Alana, I'd never actually sworn before. I'd heard people swear; James and his friends conversed almost exclusively in expletives, but I'd never joined in. It occurred to me, though, that my lack of enthusiasm was a direct result of my mother's view that swearing was vulgar. It then occurred to me that my mother wasn't present.

'Bullshit,' I signed. Alana nodded and I sat up a bit straighter, suddenly desperate to make her smile like I'd done before. 'So, what's the sign for bitch?' I succeeded.

As she grinned, Alana curled the fingers of each of her hands up, as if she was going to sign the letter 'b', then made them collide, one hand moving up and the other down.

For the next hour, we sat there together. Alana taught me every obscenity she knew, as well as basic conversational phrases. Her and her mum had joined a sign language class at the community centre near their old house, though she didn't say where that was. Alana had also taught herself bits from online tutorials. After a while, she stopped signing.

'It's probably time for tea,' she said, jumping off the couch. 'Are you going home, or do you want to stay?'

There was no doubt about what my answer was going to be. 'I'd love to stay.'

I stood up too and Alana held her hand out towards me. It took me less than a second to place my palm in hers. I didn't even consider the fact that I'd never held James' hand.

Alana took me back to her kitchen, telling me that her and her mum didn't have much food in yet, but that they had plenty of takeout menus.

'Where do you fancy going?' she asked, pointing to a corkboard on the wall that had various flyers and leaflets attached to it. 'I mean, you should know which places have good food, right?'

'Well, they don't do menus that you can take away,' I said, my mind predictably wandering to my usual eating place. I realised that our hands were still connected, and I prayed for my palm to not get sweaty. 'But there's a café just a few minutes away.' My voice trailed off as I spoke; I wasn't sure what the etiquette regarding Vellichor would be now James and I had split up. Thanks to my insistence, it had always been our go-to date location. 'We could go there.'

'Are you sure?' Alana asked, frowning a little. She looked down at our hands as I nodded, then she pulled hers away. I watched her walk back into the hall, my palm feeling uncomfortably cold.

'Yeah. It's a little old-fashioned, but the manager's a family friend.'

'Then we should go there,' she said, not quite looking at me. 'I'll just get some shoes and my key.'

As Alana sauntered upstairs, I looked around her kitchen again. I hadn't noticed my mum's basket before, but it was sitting in pride of place on the table. Several items had been taken out. Lying beside it was a reusable shopping bag, out of which two university prospectuses had fallen. I wondered where Alana was planning on going, and how likely it was that she had applied to the same places as me.

'You ready to go?' Alana asked from behind me. She was now wearing a black leather jacket and heeled boots, making her even taller. I thought about how dowdy I must look beside her, then dismissed the idea; I wanted to enjoy the rest of my time with her, not worry about my appearance.

'Yeah, sure.' We walked out of the house and down the eerily quiet street. I knew that, in just a few weeks, there'd be kids playing all down the road and in their gardens, shrieking as if it was their life's purpose to prevent silence from settling. 'It's called Vellichor,' I said, as we neared the cafe. 'It's actually one of my favourite places.'

A flicker of recognition seemed to cross Alana's face as I pushed open the door, explained immediately by the presence of Mrs Wilson.

'Alana?' She bustled over. 'Are you okay?' Judging by the way her hands moved, I assumed she was signing as she spoke. I made a mental note to remember the gestures she performed.

'Yeah, I'm fine,' Alana said and signed simultaneously. She glanced over to me. 'We were hungry, and Emily said this place was good.' I couldn't believe how quickly her hands moved.

'And Miss Emily is right as always!' said Mr Costas, who had been clearing a table a few feet away. The café was quiet, as usual, though I counted at least six other customers. That was an improvement. 'Now come, come, I shall take you to your chairs.' Alana smiled at Mrs Wilson as we were led to a table near the romance section of the shop. I could feel my hands getting sweaty, almost like a late reaction to my contact with Alana before. 'What can I get you?'

I pointedly ignored the red hearts decorating the shelves beside us, as I wondered whether or not Mr Costas knew about James and me. I reflected on the way I'd stormed out of the shop, realising that I probably couldn't have made what had happened more obvious.

'Some chips and scampi please, Mr Costas,' I said, trying to discreetly wipe my hands on my legs.

'And for the lady?' He turned to Alana, who grinned and pulled her tongue out at me.

'I'll have the same, please.' She handed him the menus off the table that neither of us had even glanced at. 'With lots of salt.'

'Lots of salt,' Mr Costas repeated, nodding. He walked away, stopping by each table to check on the other customers.

Alana looked up at the shelf next to us. 'This place is really cool,' she said, her eyes scanning the book titles. 'I can see why you like it.'

'Yeah, I come here all the time,' I replied, trying to follow her gaze. 'Although I guess now your mum works here, you won't want to come back in a hurry?' I hoped I was wrong.

'Oh no, that doesn't bother me at all.' She smiled, reaching up and pulling out a novel. 'We're really close. I'm just glad she's found somewhere as great as this to work.'

The book, some wartime love story, had several crumpled pages and a slightly torn cover. Its spine had been bent multiple times. I always felt conflicted seeing novels in that condition; part of me mourned for how they must have looked when they'd just been printed, whereas another part appreciated just how well loved they must have been. Alana flicked through the first few pages to get to the title one, and she held it out to me proudly, as if she were the first person in the world to ever read what it said.

'Look!' She tapped a small handwritten message at the top of the page and I leant forward to read it, ignoring how close I was to her chest area.

'My Ellie, this is the novel you asked for back in May. I wish I was there to read it with you, and I hope it's worth the wait. Love, your Sam.' When I'd finished reading it aloud, I shrugged at Alana. 'So, what? It's hardly a great romantic poem.'

'Aren't you intrigued?' she asked, reading the message herself. 'Who were they? Were they married? Having an affair? How long ago was this written?' She replaced the book with a triumphant smile. 'I think books with dedications are the best of all.'

Alana was in the right place; most of Vellichor's donations had little dedications doodled in them.

'I bring your food,' Mr Costas announced suddenly, setting our plates down in front of us. He retrieved several sachets of salt out of his apron pocket. 'And I will get you some water, on the house.' He winked as we thanked him.

'So, do you think you're going to learn more sign language?' Alana asked, after Mr Costas brought our drinks. 'Now that you know the essentials, of course.'

'Definitely!' I ripped open a salt packet as Alana did the same. I wondered if I sounded a bit too enthusiastic. 'I mean, I really like colours, so I'll probably learn how to sign them.'

'Which colour's your favourite?'

My first thought was red-orange: the same shade as Alana's hair. My second was pink: a light salmon pink like her lips. I blinked suddenly; asking myself since when had my favourite colours been associated with another person.

'I guess all of them,' I said after a beat. 'I think every colour is beautiful.'

'Even beige?' Alana raised her eyebrows as she speared a chip with her fork.

'Yes, even beige! Brown in general is a severely underrated colour.' Alana started to eat, still looking unconvinced. 'Brown gives us chocolate and trees and...' I faltered as she leaned closer.

'And your eyes.'

If someone told me my heart stopped beating upon hearing those words, I would have believed them. 'Pardon?'

'Your eyes.' Alana sat back and opened another salt packet. 'They aren't all brown, but they definitely have some in there. They're beautiful.'

'Thanks,' I said, my voice making it sound more like a question. I remembered how, just a few hours ago, I'd been admiring her eyes in her hallway, yet that moment already felt like it happened a lifetime ago.

'I've never known anybody to like every colour,' she said, as if she hadn't just taken my breath away with a simple comment. 'Most people have at least one they can't stand. Usually yellow if not beige.'

'Oh no, I love yellow,' I said immediately, unsurprised when Alana began to chuckle. 'One of the walls in my bedroom is painted yellow.'

'Like a feature wall?'

'Kind of. My mum hates it, but I like how happy a colour it is.' As I spoke, I looked down at my hands and realised I'd been accompanying my words with enthusiastic hand gestures. I clasped my palms together and looked back at Alana, hoping she wasn't embarrassed by my over-excitement.

She smiled at me. That was a good sign. 'You seem very passionate about this.'

'I paint a lot,' I said, conscious that I didn't want to mention my new canvas with Alana's face on.

'You're an artist?'

'I guess.' I didn't mention the art degree I was due to start studying a few months later; I didn't want to ruin the moment with the thought of us being apart so soon after meeting. 'But anyway, what's your favourite colour?'

'Blue,' she replied without hesitating. 'Teal, turquoise, sapphire. I like every shade, every name.'

'Is that why?' I gestured to her ears, remembering her blue hearing aid. There was a slight pause, before Alana brought her hand up to her ear and her gaze dropped downwards.

'Oh, yeah.' She untucked her hair so it covered her ears. 'What's your favourite sound?'

'My favourite sound? I've never really thought about that.'

'That's not a surprise; you've never had to imagine hearing it for the last time.' Though Alana spoke lightly, I noticed the shift in her tone. Most notably, how her voice almost broke on her last two words. Before I could offer any sort of apology, she continued. 'Are there any sounds you like?'

I paused for a second. 'I guess I like the noise fire makes,' I said, thinking back to my annual camping trips with my dad. 'The crackling sound always makes me feel sleepy and safe. Plus, it reminds me of the smell and that's gorgeous.'

Alana laughed a little and I wondered if I was being too pedantic. She spoke before I had time to ask. 'You know, I actually love the sound of water. Be that rain, or the ocean's waves. I think that's why I love the colour blue so much; it helps me remember my favourite sounds.'

'Well, you know what they say,' I began, my mouth moving before my brain could tell it not to. 'Opposites attract.'

Alana looked away then, as I tried to work out why the hell I'd said that. She popped a chip in her mouth instead of replying, then began to sign. I turned around and saw she was trying to say something to Mrs Wilson, who promptly nodded.

'I was asking for more salt,' she explained to me after swallowing, moving the conversation away from the awkward pause.

'Ah.' Whilst I waited for one of us to speak, I began to wonder how different my life would have been, not if I was going deaf, but if I'd been born with the ability to not come across like a complete idiot in every conversation.

'Alana!' Mrs Wilson chastised playfully when she reached our table. She took out a few salt packets from her apron pocket. 'How many times have I told you not to talk with your mouth full?'

I laughed despite myself, but Alana just looked, unblinking, at Mrs Wilson.

'As many times as it takes until it's funny?' she said. Her tone was just as light-hearted as her mum's.

'Is your food okay?' Mrs Wilson asked, serious all of a sudden. 'I'm really worried something will go wrong as it's my first day.'

'It's great, Mum,' said Alana, adding even more salt to her chips. 'Trust me.'

'I always do.' She smiled and walked over to a couple who were sitting a few tables away from us.

'Alana, why did you move here?' I asked after a second, aware that Mrs Wilson never explained. I hoped she didn't mind the question.

'There was nothing back there for us anymore,' she said simply, watching as her mum joked with a set of customers. 'We waited until I finished school, then we sold the house and set off for a change of scenery.' She brought some scampi up to her lips.

'Well, I'm glad you did move here.'

'Me too.'

Chapter 4

The smell of takeaway noodles and crispy duck teased my nostrils as I opened the front door. I kicked my shoes off and followed the smell into the kitchen.

'Do you want any of this, or did you eat with the Wilsons?' asked my mum, forgoing any traditional greetings as she filled a plate with food. She had changed her breakfast apron for one she usually reserved for Halloween; it was decorated with a picture of a pancake cut into the shape of a ghost. It also displayed the word *'crêpey'*, sewn with glow-in-the-dark thread.

'I ate with them, thanks. Alana and I went to Vellichor after having some post-break-up ice cream.' I got a drink from the fridge and joined my dad, who was already sitting at the table.

'It was nice of them to get that in for you,' my mum said, sitting down opposite me. She had a strange smile on her face. 'That's really thoughtful.'

'What? We always have ice cream in the freezer, so why wouldn't they?'

'We wouldn't do if we'd moved in the day before,' said my dad, his mouth half-full. 'That's not something you'd want to put in a moving van.' My mum nodded as I sat back, considering what they were saying. I hadn't even thought it was odd that Alana had ice cream ready, despite having a house full of boxes. I wondered what could have distracted me so much that I didn't see anything slightly weird about it.

'Yeah, well, I guess they are really nice.' I regretted echoing my mother's adjective the second I did it; for the first time, I understood why English teachers banned the word 'nice'. The term was not adequate to describe the Wilsons. I had known them for less than twenty-four hours and I already knew that.

'In that case, you could always invite them round for family game night,' suggested my dad after a few seconds. My mum nearly choked on her rice.

Family game night was a huge deal in our house; it happened once a week without fail and had done so for as long as I could remember. Even if one of us had been ill for an entire week, my mum would insist we all join in with whatever game had been chosen on the designated night. Once on a school trip to Belgium, I thought I was off the hook. My parents then made me video chat with them so we could play twenty questions. Proposing that we invite someone new to join in the tradition was like suggesting we request an invite to the next royal wedding.

'That's funny,' said my mum, her voice monotonous. 'Imagining someone who isn't family joining family game night.'

My dad smirked like he often did when he was about to get his own way. 'It'll be a nice change, Sarah,' he said, reaching out and patting my hand. 'And it's wonderful that you and Alana got along so well today, Emily. Tell her she's welcome over here any time.' His tone wasn't quite patronising, but it was something. It was something that shouldn't have been present in a conversation about Alana; she was so much more than someone to be pitied.

'They liked the basket by the way,' I said, desperate to move on to a new topic. 'And Alana's not allergic to gluten.'

'They really liked it?' My mum's sour face broke out into a grin, and my dad laughed as she gave him a look that just screamed *'I told you so.'* Their small exchange distracted me for a moment, making me wonder where Alana's dad was; I knew that few people were as lucky as me in regards to still having both parents, but he might well be due to move in with them soon. As curious as I was, I vowed never to mention him unless she did.

'Well, either that, or they chucked half of the food out,' I said, holding back a grin of my own at my mum's horrified reaction

That night, I sat at my desk and found some sign language videos on my laptop. After checking I remembered everything I'd done with Alana, I learnt some new nouns and conjunctions. It was nearly midnight and I was yawning every few seconds, but Alana still hadn't gone to bed. I was trying to keep my eyes open so I could watch an instructor sign various animals, when I saw her light turn on. She walked over to her window wearing a pair of plaid pyjama trousers and a baggy t-shirt. Her hair was damp and curly, though she looked just as mesmerising as she had done all day. She saw me looking and waved, so I stood up hurriedly. I accidentally knocked the desk with my hip.

'Good evening,' I signed. I whispered simultaneously, whilst also trying to forget the pain in my side. 'I learnt animals.' Alana responded immediately, her hands moving a lot faster than mine had done. I shook my head to show I wasn't following.

'T-h-a-t i-s g-r-e-a-t,' she spelt with her fingers, exaggeratedly mouthing the phrase.

I brought my palm up to my mouth and pulled it away to sign 'thank you'. I really wished I was in the same room as her then, just so I could see her up close.

'You're welcome,' she replied, before spelling out that she was tired. As seeing Alana had somehow managed to wake me up, I couldn't help but feel disappointed that we'd hardly spoken and she was already going to bed. Nevertheless, I waved as she closed her curtains and then I did the same with my blinds.

After I turned my laptop off, my eyes wandered over to my canvas of Alana. I debated adding to it to make myself more tired, then thought back to what she'd said in Vellichor. From behind my wardrobe, I took a smaller blank canvas than the one I was already using, and I set it on the same sheet. With small, delicate strokes of my brush, I painted a first layer with different shades of dark blue. When that was done and starting to dry, I got to work adding more detail to Alana's portrait.

Now I'd seen Alana up close, I realised just how difficult capturing the full essence of her on a canvas was going to be; she was a lot more than just a girl with lovely hair looking out of a window. Thinking back to how animated she had been whilst we watched the film at her house, I began with her freckles, lightly pencilling them on top of her nose, and I tried to draw the slight curl of her top lip that made her look permanently content. There was something still not right, however, but, before I could put my finger on what it was, I drifted off to sleep.

My dad found me the next morning with the pencil still in my hand, and I woke up as he walked over.

'You always used to be the early riser in the family,' he said, sitting on the bed beside where I was leaning. He gestured towards my canvases. 'I'm guessing you were painting during the night again.'

'Yeah, I was trying to tire myself out.' I brushed over the fact that I'd just wanted to see Alana and then think about her for longer.

My dad smiled. 'It worked, then.' He stood up and opened my blinds, revealing that Alana had already opened her curtains. I wondered why he was in his pyjamas, then realised it was his day off. 'Are you going next door again today?'

I stood up too and brushed myself down. 'Maybe,' I said, searching through my wardrobe for some clothes. 'Why? Like, why would you think I would?'

'Because I have eyes,' he said, walking towards my door. 'And your artwork has always been very realistic.' As he left my room, I heard him shout something about how he knew Alana and I would be good friends.

'Friends,' I repeated quietly, rubbing the sleep out of my eyes. I liked the idea of being friends with Alana. I grabbed a pair of black leggings and a blue t-shirt dress and got dressed, away from the window, before looking to see if Alana was visible. After seeing nothing move in her room for a while, I went downstairs to join my parents for breakfast.

'So, what's the plan for today, Emily?' my mum asked as she handed me a box of cereal. She had her Elton John apron on again.

'I'm not sure yet,' I replied, pouring myself a bowl. 'Although I was considering branching out and maybe becoming a pole dancer, you know.'

'Stripping is where the money is,' said my dad from the table as he smothered a piece of toast in peanut butter. 'Plus, it's a lot less strenuous.'

'You're not wrong.' I sat at the island, wanting to avoid the disgusting peanut smell. 'Good morning, by the way, Dad.'

'I didn't get a good morning!' my mum protested. She handed my dad the jam before he could ask for it. 'And I'm your mother; I should be your favourite.'

'There are no favourites in this family,' I said, whilst pouring milk into my bowl. 'Except when it comes to me, because I am both of yours' favourite.'

My parents hummed at each other before looking at me mock-pityingly.

'But you're leaving us for university,' said my dad, slicing his toast. 'You're leaving us to fend for ourselves, getting older and weaker every day.'

Before I could argue that my parents were the ones who wanted me to apply for university in the first place, my mum spoke again.

'Is Alana moving away for university? I never asked Linda.'

At her words, I felt myself go cold. Sure, I'd seen Alana's university brochures, but I hadn't considered her moving away so soon after coming to Kellerwick. I pushed my cereal away, no longer hungry. 'I don't know.'

'You could always ask her today,' my mum continued. 'If you're seeing her, that is.'

I nodded, managing a small smile at the thought of Alana being next door, for now at least, where I could theoretically visit her any time.

When I finished eating, I made my way back upstairs and added some more detail to my painting for Alana. When I went to get a new paintbrush from my desk, I noticed her in her bedroom. She was perched on her windowsill, looking down at the fence separating our houses. I stood in her eyeline and waved with huge arm movements, hoping to catch her eye. There was a new picture frame hanging on her wall, and a wardrobe that I hadn't noticed before. After a few seconds of me peering into her room, Alana finally saw me and waved back. She then picked up her phone and pressed it against the glass.

I shrugged and moved my finger from side to side to sign 'what?'

Alana put her phone down and made an 'o' shape with her fingers, so I did the same back to her. With the same hand, she changed her finger position to make a gun shape, causing me to shake my head. She held up seven fingers. Presuming I was being given a phone number, I sat at my desk and typed it into my phone. When I had eleven digits, as well as a thumbs up from Alana, I sent a text to the number, consisting of two question marks. The response was immediate.

Emily, hey! Are you free today?

I nodded enthusiastically from my window.

Do you want to come out with my mum and me? We're just picking up new hearing aids, but you'll know the shopping centre better than us.

Yeah, sure ☺. I replied, not even thinking about saying no. Almost certain that I had an embarrassingly big smile on my face, I ducked down slightly so I was just out of view of the window. *What time?* It took her a few minutes to reply and I used the time to get my facial muscles somewhat under control.

Now?

Right now?

Her response came in the form of a knock at the door. I looked back into Alana's room and, sure enough, she wasn't there.

'Emily, it's for you!' my mum called from downstairs. I ran down to see Alana standing beside my parents, fiddling with a necklace she was wearing. She smiled when she saw me.

'Is it okay if Emily comes shopping with us, please?' she asked them. As she turned it from side to side, I noticed that the charm around her neck was a tiny dolphin. 'We'd love to take her with us.'

'That's more than okay,' said my dad, taking a sip from the mug in his hand. Despite his baby blue slippers and the sleep in his eyes, he still had a commanding air about him and I hoped Alana wasn't feeling intimidated. 'Just have her back by midnight. Or don't.'

'Dad!'

'Oh, we will,' Alana replied, her hands now relaxed by her sides. 'Of course, we're only using her as a sat-nav.'

'Alana!'

My dad chuckled and lifted his mug up to her, clearly having appreciated the joke. At least, I thought it was a joke. Unless Alana didn't really want to spend time with me after all. I told myself I was being paranoid and brought myself back into the moment, just as Alana started to compliment my mum.

'I love your apron by the way, Mrs Davis.'

Mum looked down as if to check which one she was wearing and promptly beamed. 'You do? I had this one printed specially.'

'It's great. You should have one made with Billy Ray Cyrus talking about his Achey Bakey Tart next.' My mum laughed and that was it. In a matter of seconds, Alana had won both of my parents over, something James had never managed. 'Are you ready, Emily?' she continued. 'My mum's in the car.'

'Oh, a sat-nav is always ready.' I kissed both of my parents on their cheeks before closing the door behind us. Alana and I walked down the driveway.

'Hi Emmy,' Mrs Wilson said, turning around to look at me as I climbed into the back of the car with Alana. 'I'm glad you could make it.'

'I'm glad too,' I said, fastening my seatbelt. 'Thank you for having me.'

Their car was immaculate considering it had probably carried a bunch of stuff during their move, and it smelt like Christmas. Alana caught me sniffing and grinned.

'It's an amber and smoke air freshener,' she explained. 'It was the closest thing we had to a fireside smell.' Mrs Wilson turned back around and started to drive as I nodded, touched that Alana had remembered what I said about fire.

'It's really nice.' I waved to my parents, who were standing by the front door, before I began to sign to Alana. 'And I learnt more sign language last night.'

'What words?'

'Portrait, canvas, and brush,' I signed, saying each word aloud as I did so. 'I also learnt animals and colours.' I was increasingly amazed at how quickly I could learn BSL; even though I could remember bits of Gaelic my dad had taught me, I'd been pretty useless in my French and Spanish classes in school. 'I also learnt some school related words.'

'That's really good, well done!'

I was unnaturally thrilled at Alana's praise. 'Thank you.'

'Have you ever heard of a sign name?' she signed, speaking simultaneously. I noticed Mrs Wilson look at us in the rear-view mirror and smile.

'I haven't.'

'It's like a nickname. A boy at the community centre explained them to me. It's given to you by someone who's hard of hearing, so your name doesn't have to be spelled out all the time.'

I pointed forward, then turned my right hand on its side before bringing it down on my left palm. I then tried to remember what the sign for 'cool' was. When it wouldn't come to me, I settled for bringing my right fingers together and touching my mouth before opening my hand again, as if I were a chef who had just perfected a recipe. 'That's really lovely.'

Alana looked at me for a few seconds. 'I think I have an idea of what yours could be.'

We practised more signs in between me giving Mrs Wilson directions, stopping only when we pulled into the ground floor of the shopping centre's car park.

'We're here!' Linda exclaimed brightly. 'Thanks for the help, Emmy.'

'It was no problem.'

As we climbed out of the car, I saw Mrs Wilson switch off an actual sat-nav that was sitting on the dashboard. Before I could bring it up though, Alana looped her arm through mine and started walking.

'Which way is the pharmacy?' she asked. It took me a minute to respond; I was too busy thinking about how close we were, whilst also trying not to bump into her.

'It's just through here,' I said, pointing to the iron door that was just to the right of where we were walking. I checked that Mrs Wilson had caught up with us. 'There's a lift that takes us up to a bridge. We cross that, and all the shops surround a food court.'

'Food sounds promising.'

'Al, we need your hearing aids before we get food,' said Mrs Wilson. She held the door open for us. 'But you and Emmy can do whatever you want after we've got them.'

'Thank you, mother dearest.'

The lift arrived mere seconds after we pressed the button for it. We all walked inside, and Mrs Wilson told me how she'd registered online with the pharmacy. I was too busy looking at Alana and mine's reflection in the lift mirror to pay her a lot of attention, though; our arms were still connected, and Alana didn't seem to be in a hurry to change that. I was so distracted that I didn't even have my usual *ohnothisliftmightbreakandwe'llallbestuck* panic.

'This is it,' I said, when the lift stopped. We walked to the pharmacy and followed Mrs Wilson to an employee.

'I'm here to pick up new hearing aids for my daughter,' she began, taking a prescription out of her bag. 'Our old doctor sent the results of her latest test over. It's Alana Wilson.'

'That's great, follow me.' The man looked to be in his mid-twenties, and he wore a silver earring and had hints of blue in his brown shoulder length hair; he looked like he belonged in a band, not a pharmacy. He made his way over to the desk at the back of the shop and started to type on the old computer. 'For behind your ears, right?' He directed that question at Alana.

'Yes, please.'

'I'll go and collect those now, then.' Before he went through the door behind him, he gestured towards a display on one of the walls. 'We have a promotion on now, so you can choose a free case to take with you too.'

'Oh, thank you!' Alana hurried over to the stand, taking me with her, and we examined the different cases that were on display.

'What colour do you want? I asked her, personally liking a rainbow-coloured one the most.

'You can choose.'

'Are you sure?' Alana nodded, causing a warm, almost proud feeling in me. I didn't know why she wanted me to choose the case, but, for some reason, it meant a lot that she did. Stepping closer to the stand, I tried to find one I knew she'd like. On the third row, I found it. It was the only one without a black zip, as it was navy instead, and the case itself was decorated with light and dark blue swirls. I took it off the shelf and offered it to her. 'This one?'

She smiled and took it out of my hand. 'It's perfect, thank you.'

We walked back over to Mrs Wilson, arms still attached, and Alana handed the case to the employee. He put the small cardboard box he was holding inside it, then placed it in a little pink bag which he handed to Linda.

'Come back if you have any problems,' he said, signing as he did so. Alana let out a small gasp, and she unlinked our arms to sign back. Although I was upset at the break in contact, I wouldn't have had it any other way; her eyes had lit up, and her cheeks had lifted slightly.

Then, more than ever, I was determined to excel at learning sign language.

'I'm going to do some food shopping,' said Mrs Wilson after we walked out, her gaze directed at the map in front of us. 'We could meet up here in an hour?'

'Yes, please Mum,' said Alana, a smile still on her face. 'We'll just go and have a wander.' She turned to me as Mrs Wilson walked in the direction of the supermarket. 'Where's best to do that?'

'There's a bookshop I like,' I began, hoping Alana hadn't just humoured me the day before, and that she did genuinely like reading. 'I know I probably appear to be really boring, but I just like the atmosphere of places with books.'

'You're not boring, I promise. Which way is the bookshop?' Using the map, I showed how it was just a few shops away. Something in me was desperate to take her arm in mine again as we walked, but I resisted. Instead, I began to point out the odd, partly hidden Christmas decorations that had been left behind back in January and never taken down.

'Is that a photo booth?' Alana asked suddenly, turning my attention away from a lone purple bauble suspended from the ceiling.

'I think so.'

'We should go in!'

I ignored the fact that I hated having my photo taken, and I ignored how much I disliked small, dark spaces, and I followed Alana into the booth, closing the curtain behind us. Inside, it was even smaller than I'd expected it to be, and a tiny silver screen was the only source of light. As if the machine sensed our presence, a message popped up telling us to insert some money.

'I'm sure I have some change,' I said, trying to unzip my jacket pocket without elbowing Alana. The booth seemed to be shrinking as I dug deeper, trying to pick up the coins, and my leg was feeling uncomfortably warm against Alana's. My hot breath was making the situation worse.

'I've got it,' she replied, taking the money out of a pocket in her skirt. She put it in the machine before I could protest. A few seconds later, a countdown began on the screen. 5.

'What do we do?' I asked quickly, my mind going blank. 4. Was I meant to pose? 3. To just smile? 2. To pull tongues? 1. I tried to smile, but a bright flash from the camera made me jump and turn to Alana. I felt myself squint as my lips twisted into a grimace.

'You just don't do that,' Alana said, before laughing. I could barely see her now the flash had gone again, but my leg was starting to feel more relaxed next to hers. 'For the next one, we could pose.'

Unsure of what else to do, I went to stick two fingers up behind Alana's head in the 'bunny ears' kind of way. As I did, however, my hand collided with her arm.

'Have you stolen my idea?' I asked, as Alana withdrew herself. I quickly remade the 'v' shape behind her.

'Nope; it was definitely mine first.' There was another flash, revealing that Alana was smiling at me. I knew I was smiling too. 'Peace signs for the next one?'

I obliged willingly, suddenly oblivious to the fact the booth was too hot and the seat too small for the two of us. I turned back to the camera, ready with a smile. After the flash, Alana put her arm around me.

'Let's make this last one cute,' she said. 5 seconds. I nodded, even though she couldn't see me, and I didn't have the faintest idea about how to be *cute*. 4. Her arm on my shoulders was making me even warmer, but it felt like it belonged there. 3. I bared my teeth in a smile. 2. I felt a small amount of pressure on my cheek. It was ever so slightly damp, and I tried to keep my face composed, telling myself I had imagined it. 1. Flash.

The pressure left again, and the machine whirred as it spat out two photo strips. Alana handed me one and I stepped out of the booth to look at it, immediately missing the feeling of being pressed against her. The first picture was about as unflattering as it could possibly be; my face somehow resembled a squashed-up cereal box. Alana, however, looked beautiful. The second and third photos were nice enough, with both of us smiling, but the fourth revealed that I hadn't imagined something touching me. It showed me smiling to the camera, if slightly uneasily, and Alana kissing my cheek, her eyes closed.

'You okay?' Alana asked, holding her own photo strip. I wondered if I should bring it up; if I was supposed to, or if kiss cheeking was completely normal for friends. Instead, I chose to smile.

'Yeah. I'm great.' We walked to the bookshop, passing a sparse tinsel garland and a shop window still decorated with fake snow. 'And here we are.'

A smell of coffee and new books drifted out of the open doors, and I pointed out one last blue bauble before we went inside. Every shelf was identical and stacked neatly, the exact opposite of those in Vellichor, and the place was full of customers. As I walked over to the café section, I saw there was one spare table.

'Do you still like the sound of food?' I asked, motioning to the empty seats. 'It's more expensive than Mr Costas' shop, but we could share a muffin?'

'I'd love that.' Alana sat down as I placed an order at the counter, inhaling the intoxicating smell of a bookshop that hadn't been defiled by James' scent.

When I returned to Alana with the muffin and two bottles of water, she was typing on her phone.

'Is everything okay?'

She put her phone away quickly and smiled. 'Everything's great, and thank you.' I tried to imagine who she had been messaging, and began to wonder again what exactly she had left behind when she'd moved: whether she really did have a boyfriend, and whether he'd be visiting any time soon. I also found myself wishing I had the nerve to ask her. 'I much prefer the place where my mum works, though,' she said, picking off a bit of muffin. 'Especially as the guy who owns it seems really sweet; he let her have today off with no notice because my prescription came through sooner than expected.'

'Mr Costas is really kind like that,' I agreed, trying some of the muffin too. 'He's a family friend and I've never known him to be anything but lovely.'

'Isn't he worried about places like this putting him out of business? Like, with rent and stuff?' Alana asked, resting her chin in her hands. 'Second-hand bookshops and little cafes don't really make a lot, do they?'

'He owns it.' I thought back to when Mr Costas had officially become the owner of Vellichor. I'd only been about nine, but I remembered how he'd hosted a big party for the town and let all of us kids choose a book for free. Mine had been *Matilda,* and I had treasured it ever since. 'He started working there part-time when he moved here, and the old owner left it to him after he died.'

Before Alana could respond, I sensed someone standing near us. I looked up to see familiar floppy blond hair and tanned skin. I felt my throat tighten and my eyes burned as I looked into his.

'Emily?'

'James. What are you doing here?'

Alana had just taken a drink of water and I could see her struggling to swallow it. James looked over to her and narrowed his eyes slightly.

'I was looking for Scott; I'm meant to be meeting him somewhere near here.' I pretended like I knew who that was. 'Who's this?'

'Alana Wilson,' she said, after finally managing to swallow. She stuck out her hand for him to shake. 'I'm Emily's new neighbour.'

'You live near my house, then.' James took her hand and brought it up to his lips. 'Enchante.'

I scoffed slightly and, judging by her raised eyebrows, Alana was resisting doing the same. She pulled her hand away and reached out for the muffin again, causing James to look back at her with a slight frown; he wasn't used to girls not fawning over him.

He cleared his throat. 'Anyway, Emily. I'm glad I bumped into you; I'm having a party at my house tomorrow. Do you want to come?'

I opened my mouth to decline the offer; even if I was trying to be less predictable, I wasn't about to agree to attending my ex's party. James, however, continued to speak before I could say anything.

'Alana, you're more than welcome to come too.'

Alana looked between me and him, her expression impossible to read. On the one hand, parties and drinking and things had never appealed to me. Not at all. On the other hand, well. I couldn't actually think of anything else.

'We'd love to go,' Alana said. I widened my eyes at her.

'We would?'

'Cool. I'll see you about eight.' James put his hands in the back pockets of his jeans and sauntered out. I carried on looking at Alana.

'He seems nice,' she said, ripping off more of the muffin and rolling it in between her fingers.

'He is, I guess.' Alana looked up, the crumb halfway to her mouth. I continued to speak, paying no attention to my words because doing so would have distracted me from her. 'Though, I saw him more as charming. You know, in that stereotypical pretty-guy-talking-to-an-unpopular-girl kind of way. I think that's why I fell for him.' Alana ate the morsel of food as I had a sip of water. 'And you really don't have to come to his party, by the way.' I didn't mention how she was the one who said we'd go.

'Don't worry, I want to.' Alana's face looked almost mischievous, and I started to pay far too much attention to the dimple that had reappeared on her cheek. 'As long as you're okay with it. Besides, I have to make sure my new bestie doesn't decide she wants to get back with her boyfriend and leave me alone all summer.'

'I would never.' The thought of being Alana's 'bestie' sent a shiver down my back, and I struggled not to react outwardly. Then, the truth of the matter hit me, and I was forced to consider the fact that I was going to my first ever proper party. I was going to see everyone I thought I'd left behind in school: the girls who used to snicker when I got changed during PE; who never picked me for projects; who were the reason why, until I met James, I'd spent all my lunchtimes in the Art department. I wondered if they'd be better with alcohol. Worse? I realised I'd started to bite my lip. I tried to tear my teeth away, but they dug in harder.

'Whoa, are you okay?' Alana asked, breaking me out of my trance. She looked me up and down. 'What's up?'

I couldn't admit I'd never been to a party before, or that I was petrified of embarrassing myself whilst I was there; I knew Alana probably thought I was enough of a loser as it was.

'I haven't... haven't got anything to wear.' At least I didn't have to lie. 'I have nothing that's suitable really.'

'We can fix that!' Alana pulled her phone back out of her pocket. She tapped her long, black painted nails on the keyboard. 'I'll just text my mum and say we might take longer than an hour.'

If it had been anybody other than Alana dragging me by my wrist through various clothes shops, I would have been beyond bored. As Alana seemed in her element though, I was secretly enjoying myself; I liked watching her gaze at the different outfits and displays we passed. When we entered the sixth shop, one that felt far too cool for the likes of me, Alana finally slowed down her pace.

'Here. Here will do.' I followed her over to a section that seemed to exclusively stock dresses. Within seconds, I found myself taken aback by the sheer amount of them on display; there were dresses of every style and every colour. The thought of rooting through that many clothes was one that crossed my mind only in nightmares.

'You know what?' I began, slowly backing away. 'I'll be fine; I'm sure I will find something at home.'

Alana put a hand on her hip. 'You are not getting away that easily.' She used her other hand to point at the various racks in front of me. 'Is it not a dress that you want? We can find you something else.'

'No, I like dresses,' I muttered, already standing beside her again. 'I just don't like spending hours trying on clothes only for none of them to fit right.'

'What are you talking about?' Alana removed several hangers and replaced them just as quickly. 'Is that what you think happens when you go shopping?'

'Basically, yeah; everything is either too long or too tight. I don't exactly have the ideal body type.' As I spoke, I became painfully aware of how self-pitying I sounded. 'It's not that big a deal, it just gets kind of boring after a while. We're never going to find me a party outfit.'

I sat down on a small, fluffy seat as Alana shook her head.

'That, my dear Emily, is where you are wrong.' She left the dress section and went to speak to one of the shop assistants. I tucked my legs underneath me, conscious of how out of place I probably looked. When I was with Alana, I was okay; she looked like she belonged anywhere, and I could fool myself into believing I did too. Without her, however, I was just a short geeky girl who had been in more clothes shops in the last ten minutes than in the last ten years.

After what felt like hours, during which several girls from school walked past me without seeing me, Alana returned. She had a folded black garment in her hand and she presented it grandly, bowing ever so slightly. I stood up and took it from her.

'That will do it,' she said confidently as she steered me towards the changing rooms. 'That right there will restore your faith in shopping.'

'I highly doubt that.'

'You shall see!' Alana gently pushed me into one of the cubicles and closed the curtain behind me.

Whilst avoiding looking in the mirror, I unfolded the item of clothing to see that it was a strapless jumpsuit. As I began to undress, I moaned inwardly and tried to understand how Alana, who clearly had better fashion sense than me, could think a jumpsuit would ever look right on someone like me. Nevertheless, I stepped into it and saw she had somehow guessed my exact size. Plus, when it was on, I had to admit it looked a million times better than I had expected it to.

I turned to the side, then to the other, then tried to see what it looked like from the back, and I was still impressed; it didn't make me look short or childlike like I had been expecting it to. Alana really did know what she was doing.

'Hey, are you ready?' Speak of the devil. I stood up straighter and patted my hair down.

'I'm ready.' I turned to face her as she parted the curtains and walked in. Her face broke out into a smile as she did so. I watched her look up the whole length of my body before her eyes lingered on mine.

'I knew it.' That reaction was enough to stop me from wanting to wear any other outfit ever again. I turned back to the mirror, my face suddenly feeling hot. 'Every guy at that party is going to want to kiss you.'

I could see my mouth droop a little, but I didn't understand why; it was a well-meant compliment. I think I just couldn't shake the feeling that it wasn't the compliment I'd been hoping for.

'Do you really think so?' The fact that I didn't want to kiss any boys at the party was irrelevant.

'I know so.' Alana walked up behind me so we were both looking in the mirror, and I saw our reflection for the second time that day. Even with the new outfit, I looked positively plain beside her; if her hair and eyes weren't enough, her bright blue skirt and low-cut vest top ensured she stood out from everybody else. It wasn't in a bad way, no, never in a bad way. I decided I really liked looking at myself beside her, despite how much more mediocre than normal she managed to make me look. 'If I were a boy...' she continued, before winking and heading out of the room. 'Now, you should probably put your clothes back on, so we can go and pay.'

Alana left and closed the curtain again, having said that second sentence a lot faster than the first. I felt my head beginning to reel. What did that mean? If she were a boy... what? What did I want it to mean? The more I thought about it, the more I figured I was just overthinking things; I wasn't used to having girlfriends, so I had no idea if that was the type of thing people said to each other.

Chapter 5

During the car ride home, Alana barely looked at me. Her head was turned towards her window for the first few miles, and she didn't speak until Mrs Wilson directly asked her a question.

'Al, honey, are you alright?' Linda's eyes were flickering between the rear-view mirror and the road in front of her. Her hand hovered over the indicator as if she was debating pulling over.

'Yeah, Mum, I'm fine.' Alana glanced over at me, and I tried to unclench my facial expressions and not look as concerned about her sudden silence as I felt. 'Emily's... friend invited us to a party that he's hosting tomorrow. Is it okay if I go?'

Mrs Wilson's shoulders relaxed as she went back to focusing completely on the road. 'Of course you can go,' she replied, before pausing and looking in her mirror again. 'Unless you think –'

'No, I don't. It will be great.' Before I had the chance to even consider what they were alluding to, Alana started speaking hurriedly. 'Emily bought a new jumpsuit specially.'

'So that's why you took longer.' As we stopped at a set of traffic lights, Mrs Wilson turned around and gave me a sympathetic look. 'I'm sorry you had to go clothes shopping with her; I know how torturous it can be.'

She started to drive again as Alana protested indignantly. Holding back a laugh, I could feel a rush of happiness as I considered how easily I found contributing to the conversation; I had never been so comfortable talking with two people that weren't my parents before.

As Mrs Wilson parked outside her house, I saw my mum waving at me from our living room window. Alana and I waved back as we got out of the car, and my mum was at the bottom of the drive a few seconds later.

'How was shopping?' she asked, watching as Alana and I retrieved the bags.

Mrs Wilson laughed as she fumbled with her keys. 'Something tells me Emmy dislikes clothes shopping as much as I do.'

We followed her inside, my mum closing the front door behind us.

'I guess she never has been very fond of makeshift fashion shows.' I wondered why she'd come into the Wilsons' house with us, but then saw how gleeful she looked when we reached the kitchen and she caught sight of the half-empty basket.

'I like buying new clothes,' Alana huffed playfully, starting to unpack the shopping as my mum and I stood back. 'And you have to admit you look flawless in your new outfit.'

Flawless? Me?

'New outfit?' My mum crossed her arms. 'Are you telling me you actually convinced Emily to buy clothes?'

Alana nodded and looked pointedly at the lone bag I was still holding.

I grunted loudly and held it just out of my mum's reach. 'Before you get excited, Mum, it's for a party. I only bought it because we have been invited to a party on Friday.'

'Whose party?'

'James's.' If it hadn't been for the small clunking noises of tins and jars being put in the cupboards by Mrs Wilson, we all would have been able to hear a flea fart in that moment. My mum coughed slightly.

'Oh. I'm sure that will be fun.'

I looked over at the clock, suddenly desperate for an excuse to leave. 'I'll see you tomorrow,' I said quickly when I couldn't think of one. 'Thank you for taking me with you, Mrs Wilson, and thanks for your help, Alana.' I dragged my mum out of their house before they even had the chance to reply.

'Goodbye!' called my mum.

'That wasn't awkward at all,' I said, pushing open our front door. My dad was waiting just outside the living room, having got dressed whilst I was out.

'What wasn't awkward at all?'

'Emily is going to a party,' said my mum, enunciating each individual syllable as if she was trying to understand her own words.

I groaned as I moved to sit on the sofa; I hadn't realised that everyone else thought I was predictable too. 'Is that really so hard to believe?'

They followed me into the room and Dad sat beside me as my mum perched on the edge of our armchair.

'But a party?' She still wasn't getting it. 'Emily, honey, you don't really go outside. What's got into you? Is it Alana?' I looked anywhere but at them, feeling myself grimace at what was definitely not meant to be a euphemism.

'I'm just trying to get out there a bit.' I was sure there was some truth in what I was saying, even though I didn't know where.

'And you're going to be okay seeing James again?'

'James?' My dad crossed his arms and stared hard at me. 'James will be at this party?'

'Yes, but it will be fine,' I said, unable to stop myself from waving my hands defensively. I wished the conversation could just move on to something else; sure, I was the least likely person to ever agree to go to a party, but my parents were the ones who always wanted me to at least try and have a social life. Plus, I wasn't hating my new, less predictable ways. 'And I'm going to go to my room for a bit.' I left them in the living room, probably trying to work out why I was so on edge; I wanted to know myself.

It didn't look like Alana was in her room, so I tucked my hair behind my ears and sat down on the floor with my art supplies. I stared at the canvas of her for a few minutes, trying to work out what to do to it, before I began to work on her hair. Although I'd seen it more when it was straight, I still wanted to draw it like it was when it was natural, and I ended up drawing, erasing, and redrawing the corkscrew curls over and over again. When it was done, it made the picture look more realistic than any portrait that I'd done before. I was so busy grinning at it like a fool that I didn't hear my dad come in behind me.

'That's looking really good.'

I jumped when I heard him. 'Thank you.'

He exhaled as he sat down on the floor beside me and, maybe as a result of thinking so intensely about Alana's, I noticed how thin his hair was becoming. Self-consciously, I patted my own black mop, yet it was just as thick and unruly as ever.

'Are you looking at my balding head?' He grinned, his eyes following my hand. I nodded sheepishly. 'You don't need to worry; as long as you don't become a lawyer, your hair shouldn't drop out like mine is doing at the moment.'

'Is work really bad again?' It was rare that my dad got the chance to talk about what was making him worry; my mother was a firm believer in men ignoring their problems until they went away, so him and me had to try and talk when she wasn't around. We hadn't had a venting session with each other for a long while.

'It could be worse.'

'That doesn't mean it isn't bad.'

'You're right; it doesn't.' He picked up one of my pencils and started to fiddle with it. 'So, what's the deal with this party? You aren't trying to get back together with James, are you?'

'No, I'm not. I just really like Alana and I figured it was a good excuse to spend time together.'

'That's as good a reason to socialise as any.' He tapped the pencil rhythmically against the back of his hand. 'You're not expecting me to give you a big before-your-first-party talk, are you? Just because I stopped rehearsing that when you were sixteen.'

'No, I'm not expecting it.' I wondered why he wasn't opening up like he usually would about what was getting him down, but I knew he'd find a way to talk to me if he needed to. He gave me a small smile.

'Good, good.' He heaved himself up and dropped the pencil back on the floor. 'Now, your mum has been making dinner so it's probably ready by now.' Only then, did I notice just how dark it had become outside. Thanks to summer, the sun was still partly out, but I'd been so engrossed in my drawing that I hadn't noticed how much time had passed. Right on cue, my mum called us from the kitchen.

'Sit, sit, sit,' she said, when we'd walked downstairs. She was holding a bowl of salad and a plate of onion rings. She placed them down on the table and brought over a burger for each of us. 'I was going to put the barbecue on, but I thought cooking them in the oven might be quicker.' She held out knives and forks for my dad and me to take, but we just looked at her blankly before picking up our burgers with our hands. 'Savages,' she muttered.

Chapter 6

On the day of the party, I didn't see Alana at all; her curtains remained closed until around six o'clock in the evening and, though I desperately wanted to, I resisted the urge to text her in case I seemed too clingy.

I was learning more sign language at my desk when I finally saw her. She waved at me, her hair straightened once again. I, far too enthusiastically, waved back.

'Are you getting dressed?' she signed, before tapping an imaginary watch on her wrist.

'Now?' We still had plenty of time.

Alana nodded slowly, and I tried to look at what she was wearing, only to see she had on a thin blue dressing gown.

'Are you getting dressed?' I repeated her exact actions.

Alana didn't respond, instead choosing to untie her satin belt. Although I couldn't explain why, I felt my breath hitch in my throat. I had even more difficulty breathing when she took the garment off; she revealed a white dress that stopped midway down her thigh and clung to her figure perfectly. She spun around slowly and, as the outfit got caught in the slight sunlight, I realised it was made up of hundreds of sequins.

'Now are you getting dressed?' Her smile suggested that she knew she'd caught me off guard, and I was certain I'd never seen somebody look so beautiful before. A million thoughts crossed my mind then, all of them centring on how ridiculous it was that Alana Wilson had agreed to befriend me. Suddenly, my jumpsuit seemed far too plain for the party.

I only registered that I hadn't signed back to Alana when she knocked on her window.

'Yes. Right now,' I signed.

Alana winked and closed her curtains, as if to give me some privacy.

After pulling my new outfit on and spritzing myself with some body spray, I looked at myself in my mirror. I didn't want to try messing around with make-up, seeing as I literally had no idea how to use it, but I wanted to do something that would help me look good for Alana. I took a small brush off my bedside table and attempted to tame my hair, giving up when the bristles got stuck for the third time. I checked the clock and, after seeing it was nearly eight o'clock, I opened my curtains, which I had closed shortly after Alana had done the same with hers.

She was sitting in the window waiting and, when we made eye contact, she just pointed at me. I pointed at myself too and waited for her to continue, far too excited to see what she was going to sign. Alana made a fist with her right hand, only leaving out her little finger, then made several circles on her left palm. I tried to remember seeing it before, and was somewhat certain that it meant serious. She then did the sign for beautiful, and any worries about my hair and my lack of make-up went away. In that moment, the fact that Alana thought I looked beautiful meant more to me than anything else could have.

'You ready?' she continued.

I gave her a thumbs up and grabbed my phone off my desk before slipping into the only heels I owned. I'd decided that wearing something other than my pumps would be an excellent way to continue being less predictable, and the shoes matched my grey jacket. They were also tall enough to make me look of average height, without being so tall that I couldn't walk in them.

'Emily! You look lovely,' Mum said as I came down the stairs. She was standing in the living room doorway, most likely waiting for my dad to come home, and her eyes looked almost tearful when she saw me. 'Have fun, okay? And don't let Alana feel isolated.' That was the last thing I ever wanted to do.

'I'll stay with her all night.' I gave her a small wave before opening our front door. Alana was leaving her house at the same time, and we smiled at each other as we met on the pavement.

'Who are you and what have you done with Emily Davis?' she asked, her eyes trailing down my body once again. I let my eyes do the same to hers as I marvelled at her toned legs and white stilettos. I wondered if the sight of her would always leave me breathless, and I hoped to God that it would.

'I'm a girl with a party to go to.' I started walking in the direction of James' house, having never been so nervous about doing so as I was then. 'And I never thought I'd say that.' When we reached his road, I could hear blaring pop music and see hordes of teenagers standing around in his front garden. Although the night had barely begun, my former classmates hadn't wasted any time in starting the party and, if it hadn't been for my neighbour, I would have immediately turned back around; seeing them brought back memories of school I simply didn't care to relive.

'Come on,' Alana said. She turned around to look at me, and I realised that I'd stopped moving in favour of staring at the usually serene house. I hurried to catch up with her so we could walk inside together.

After reaching the top of his driveway, we could see that James' front door was open, and we were pushed inside by a cheering gang of boys who had come up behind us. They promptly ran over to the dining room table and joined some other people, who were throwing plastic balls into cups. Alana smiled almost knowingly, and I willed myself to do the same.

We walked over to the kitchen counter. It was littered with bottles of different sizes and disposable shot glasses, as well as plastic cups in every colour. The increasingly strong smell of alcohol was worsened by a lingering scent of body odour and Doritos, and I tried my best to breathe through my mouth.

Alana picked up a red cup and half-filled it with vodka, before adding a few drops of lemonade. When she poured my drink, she did the opposite. She saw me staring and the corner of her mouth lifted slightly.

'I'm guessing this is your first time drinking alcohol,' she said, half-shouting so I could hear her over the music. 'I don't want to make you sick.'

'I'll be fine.' I picked up a bottle that had a plastic sombrero as its cap. It seemed like being around a load of people had made me want to impress Alana even more than usual; maybe because I'd never really had to fight for her attention before. Although the drink smelt vile, I poured some of that into my cup too and brought the concoction up to my lips. 'Cheers.'

'Cheers.' Alana's voice was a lot more uncertain than mine. We both took a gulp from our respective drinks, and it took everything I had to keep a straight face; obviously I'd always known that alcohol tasted bad, I just hadn't excepted it to make my throat feel like it was on fire.

'That tastes awful.'

'Emily, perhaps mixing different spirits isn't your best plan.' Alana's expression was completely unchanged, as if she had just been drinking water.

'I'll be fine,' I repeated, squeezing my eyes shut as I had another sip.

'Ladies.' A dark-haired boy, who was just a bit taller than Alana and was holding a can of cider, sauntered over to us. His half-shouting was a lot less pleasant to listen to than Alana's. 'Do either of you happen to like Chinese food?'

I looked at Alana blankly; the only food I had noticed in the kitchen was nachos, thanks to their nauseating scent, and pizza. Before I could tell him that, however, Alana patted him on his shoulder.

'Thanks for coming over here, and for... asking us that, but my friend and I were trying to have a little talk.'

'I'm good at talking.' He took a swig from his drink and shrugged so that Alana's hand fell. Then he put his arm around her waist, just as I finally began to feel a slight buzz from what I'd been drinking. It was then that I remembered how I'd always been warned against drinking on an empty stomach.

'You don't want to talk about this,' I told the boy, partly enjoying how light I was beginning to feel. Alana just carried on drinking, as if she hadn't even noticed he was touching her.

'I'm sure I do. My name's Scott.' Alana raised her eyebrows, presumably having made the same connection as me. 'So, what was it you were discussing?'

'Water infections,' I said bluntly. Tipsy me wanted to avoid the cliché use of periods, and thus continue steering away from being predictable, and UTIs were the first slightly gross thing I could come up with. Much to my chagrin, Scott didn't even bat an eyelid.

'That sounds like a cool conversation.' Alana rolled her eyes at his statement before she placed her suddenly empty cup on the table. I hurriedly finished my drink too and made up another, mixing everything that looked even slightly alcoholic. 'Hey, shouldn't you slow down there?' Scott's arm was still around Alana and she almost seemed to be leaning into him. The sight, and possibly the alcohol, turned my stomach slightly.

'It's a party!' I replied, taking a sip and immediately pursing my lips at the sour taste. 'Getting drunk is the whole point of being here.'

'In that case, I might take your friend into the back room whilst you do that. My friends and I were thinking of playing ring of fire.'

I waited for Alana to say no. I waited for her to shake him off and say she had no interest in playing whatever the hell 'ring of fire' was. She didn't.

'You'll be okay, right?' she asked, having made up another drink that was 90% vodka and 10% mixer.

Of course I wasn't going to be okay; I didn't know how to act at a party and I barely recognised anybody there. I wasn't about to risk sounding that pathetic, however.

'Of course. I'll join you guys in a bit.' Scott carted Alana off, just as James approached me from the other direction with a grin on his face.

'Emily! You actually came.'

'I did!' He wrapped his arms around me, and I inadvertently heaved as I felt him press against my stomach. 'Thanks for the invitation.' I burped after I spoke, heaving again but that time due to the smell of my breath. I clamped a hand over my mouth.

'Where's your friend?' James asked, letting go of me.

'Round there.' I gestured to the back room. I could see Alana being led to a sofa that a few boys were already sitting on. She laughed at something they said to her, and I could feel my chest tightening; I liked being the one making her laugh.

'She looks like she's having fun. Shot?'

I looked down to see that James was pouring the sombrero liquid into two of the little shot glasses. After shooting another glance at Alana, who had slightly turned her back to the other boys and was talking to Scott, I nodded.

'Shot.' It was easier to drink than I had imagined, though the taste made me scrunch my face up, and the people around us cheered as James poured out two more. He lifted one of the glasses up, his face completely clear of judgement, and I knew I could say no without it being an issue. The thing was, I didn't really want to say no. I took the drink off him and chugged it before he even had the chance to pick his up. My head was starting to feel cloudy, and I couldn't focus on any one thought for long, suddenly making the party feel like it wasn't the worst place to be after all. 'I'm going to my friend,' I told James, as I started to top my drink up with vodka. My words slurred slightly.

He took the bottle out of my hand.

'Maybe you should sit down first, Emily.' His voice was laced with concern and I hummed as I considered how caring he could be, despite him breaking up with me like he did.

'You're lovely to me,' I said, feeling slightly dizzy as I tilted my head to look up at him. 'Thank you for being lovely.'

I sauntered into the back room and sat on James' dad's rocking chair. I watched as Alana carried on speaking to Scott, who had one arm across his chest and the other resting on the back of the sofa. I couldn't see any rings around them, nor could I see any fire. Considering it was a party, I couldn't even see a deck of cards available for a normal drinking game.

After a few minutes, Alana made eye contact with me. Although she continued to talk to Scott, I saw her put her drink on the floor and start to sign discreetly. She had one hand out flat, palm facing upwards, and the other resting on top of it in the thumbs up position. She pulled her hands closer to herself, then folded them on her lap as Scott looked down.

'Help me?' I muttered, the music loud enough to drown me out. My thoughts were swimming around too quickly in my head for me to be able to make sense of the situation. I simply didn't understand why she would need help; she was Alana and Alana looked fine from what I could see. I began to understand when Scott's hand moved from its position on the sofa onto her head and he began to pet her hair, almost as if she were a dog. When Alana didn't push him off, I could feel myself getting even angrier at him.

'And do you have a boyfriend, babe?' I heard him ask, jutting out his chin as he did so.

'I can't say I do.' Alana looked down with wide eyes, and I saw that Scott's other hand was now resting on her leg, dangerously close to the hem of her dress. I stood up, finally understanding that I needed to intervene, but I had to steady myself as my legs threatened to collapse underneath me.

'Then, do you want to have some fun?' Scott moved his hand further up Alana's thigh, just as she pushed him away, her features contorted in a display of disgust. 'What the hell?'

'Don't put your hands on me like that.' Her raised voice drew the attention of everyone in the room, including the other boys on the couch. Scott looked at her, his brow creased.

'But you said you don't have a boyfriend,' he hissed.

Alana clenched her fist, as if she wanted to punch him, and all I could think was that I wanted to do the same. As much as I willed myself to get involved, however, I felt like I was frozen where I was. I started to hate myself for not stepping in sooner.

'My relationship status has nothing to do with whether or not you get to touch my body.' Her collected air was a direct contrast to her gritted teeth.

'Relax, babe.' Scott glanced around nervously, continuing when he saw that nearly everyone had gone back to their own conversations. I was still hovering near them, holding my cup and trying to force myself to speak. 'I just didn't want some boyfriend coming after me for touching you.'

Alana stood and opened her mouth, but nothing came out. I hated seeing her so helpless and, before I could register what was happening, I finally reacted to Scott's actions. Within seconds, I'd poured what was left of my drink onto his head. That drew the room's focus back to him once again.

'What are you –?'

'A word of advice,' I began, watching with satisfaction as cider and vodka and whatever else I'd put into my drink dripped down his eyes. 'Worry more about the girl you're harassing than about her possible boyfriend.' Scott got up off the couch and stood in front of me, looking down with a scowl. I took a deep breath and tried not to flinch. 'Or, better yet, just don't harass girls.'

'Emily, you don't have to –'

'I do.' Deep down, I knew standing up to a guy who was twice my size was probably not my best plan. Either the alcohol or the fact I was surrounded by so many people, however, assured me I was going to be okay.

'And who exactly are you? Her girlfriend?' Scott's sneer was enough to turn me speechless once again, as I tried desperately to think of a response. I also tried to figure out since when one girl sticking up for another girl had become something reserved only for lesbians. And why a stranger calling me Alana's girlfriend had robbed me of my ability to talk.

'She has more chance of getting with me than you do.' Alana's statement was met with a room full of wolf whistles, as well as jeers aimed towards Scott, and she took my hand as soon as she delivered it. I didn't even have time to fully register her words. 'Let's get out of here.'

We walked back through James' house silently, avoiding the couples making out in every doorway and the patches of suspiciously coloured carpet. I was horribly aware of how sweaty my palm was once again, but Alana seemed unaffected as she led me outside.

'That was horrendous,' she said as we walked down the drive. Well, she walked. I mainly stumbled.

'I'm so sorry.' I found it even harder to speak now we were alone. My conscious effort to not slur my words was in vain. 'He shouldn't have done that to you. I should have helped when you asked me to.'

'Don't worry about it. Sex-obsessed creeps will be sex-obsessed creeps.'

'But I could have done something and instead I was just drinking.' I couldn't shake the feeling that I'd let Alana down. That I shouldn't have let her walk away with a stranger, even if he was James' friend. That I should have gone with her instead of doing shots with James and that –

'It's only just nine o'clock.' Alana's observation distracted me from my thought spiral.

'Seriously?' I checked my phone, convinced she was wrong; the night felt like it had been going on forever. 'My parents will never let me live this down if I go home now.'

Alana looked at me, having brought her other hand up to her bottom lip. 'What should we do, then?'

Several teenagers passed us as they walked through James' front garden, and all I knew was that I wanted to be anywhere but there.

'We should go to the park,' I said. 'It's not far away.' I attempted to walk briskly in the right direction, finding the flat road much better for moving. I had forgotten, though, that Alana and I were still holding hands. She laughed and let me pull her along.

'You're a lot less shy when you're drunk, you know.' She squeezed my hand. 'When we met, you were the last person I could have imagined pouring a drink over someone's head.'

'Well, that creature deserved it.' Now we had left the party behind, my voice sounded horribly loud in the night air. I tried to lower it, but was conscious that Alana mightn't be able to hear a whisper. 'And I wanted to protect you.'

'Oh, you did?' Alana lowered her voice too, then. She was also grinning, however, which made me think she wasn't being as serious as I was.

'Of course I did!'

She hummed in response and, if her smile hadn't been so beautiful, I probably would have insisted she take me seriously. We walked to the park, swinging our hands together and lifting them over each bin we passed so we didn't have to let go of each other. If someone had told me we weren't the only people in the world that night, I wouldn't have believed them.

'We should go to the children's bit,' I said, starting to run through the park gates. My voice's volume had risen again. 'We can sit on the swings!'

'I love swings.' I suspected that Alana was just humouring me, but she was running with me and she was laughing, so I didn't care. I was so busy watching her that I nearly ran straight into a tree. 'Oh my God, are you okay?'

'Whoops.' I giggled and ran my fingers through my hair, before walking towards the play area. 'I'm not okay; I'm Emily.'

Alana tutted as we made our way to the swing set and sat down beside each other. She started to swing gently, forcing me to do the same as our hands were still together. The park was the best place to see stars, and I looked at them as we swung.

'I love watching the sky at night,' I said.

'What was that, sorry?'

I turned my gaze onto Alana, and I knew I never needed to look up again; in the dim moonlight, her eyes looked as if they were sparkling, and no number of stars could ever have bettered that.

'It doesn't matter.' My voice was hoarse as I looked at her, almost like I wanted to sear the image of her into my brain. She cleared her throat and looked away, inadvertently shattering my heart a little. As my head started to spin again, I considered the fact that I had probably had too much to drink. 'So. You don't have a boyfriend?' It had taken me up until that moment to fully register what she'd said to Scott at the party and, probably thanks to the copious amounts of alcohol, I was weirdly happy about it.

'No, I don't.' She still wasn't looking at me and I tried to figure out if I had upset her by watching her so intently; I didn't think I had stared that much. The thought that I'd made Alana uncomfortable, especially when paired with the swinging motion, made me feel sick. Truly, physically sick. I let go of her hand and jumped off the swing before stumbling over to one of the park bins. I only just made it in time to empty my stomach.

'Ew.'

'Crap. Emily, it's okay.' I felt two hands pulling my hair off my face as I spluttered some more, my throat once again feeling like it was on fire. The action sobered me up a little and I realised just how much I was probably repulsing Alana.

'I'm sorry,' I said, stepping away from her. The smell of spirits and cider was overwhelmingly strong, and I sat back down on the swing, annoyed at myself for being such an embarrassment.

'It's fine.' Alana sat beside me again.

'Thanks.' I pushed my feet off the floor and set the swing in motion, hoping the movement wouldn't make me sick again. I wondered if I was drunk enough to wake up the next day having forgotten what I'd just done. It wasn't long until Alana started to swing too, managing to get a lot higher than me.

'Are you okay?'

'Are you?' I deflected, truly not knowing how I was feeling. A part of me wanted to go back to the party and tell Scott exactly what I thought of him; part of me wanted to go home and sleep; no part of me wanted to leave Alana. 'Because I'd understand if you weren't.' I wondered what I was supposed to say to somebody who'd just been assaulted, and I wished I knew what could make her feel better.

Alana pushed her legs out to slow down, and soon our swinging became synchronised. 'I'm okay. Honestly.' In that moment, that was all I needed to hear.

We stayed on the swings for over an hour, simply admiring the sky, and I loved how the night felt like it was ours. I knew Alana was there, and she knew I was too, and for some reason that was enough. It wasn't until we began the journey home that she spoke again.

'I'm hopefully having surgery in a few weeks,' she told me, her breath creating clouds in the light breeze. It made her words look like they were magic.

'You are?' Although I was feeling decidedly less drunk, I still wasn't enunciating very clearly. I hoped Alana could understand me.

'At the end of July. Have you ever heard of cochlear implants?'

As I tried to talk, I heard a sharp, barking laugh escape my lips. 'You said cock,' I said, unable to stop myself.

Alana pursed her lips. 'I. I guess I did. Regardless, my old doctor suggested the procedure before we moved. It's to stimulate my hearing nerve.' She was using too many words for me to follow completely, but I nodded just as I caught my foot on a loose paving stone.

'Whoops! Well, it's worth a try.'

'Everything's worth a try,' Alana replied. She had grabbed my arm before I could fall. 'Are you alright?'

'Of course! And look, I tried going to a party and I tried drinking, so you should try your implants.' I knew I had begun to ramble, but I was too busy concentrating on the dull throbbing sensation in my toes to stop. 'Although maybe that didn't work out so well. After all, I hardly saw you at the party and then that guy was a jerk and I was just watching you both when I wanted to be sitting with–' I brought my hand up to my mouth, unsure of where I was going with my statement, but conscious that perhaps I should quit while I was ahead.

'You wanted to be sitting with who?' Alana probed. I brought my hand back down. 'With Scott?'

'No! No. Definitely no.' I shuddered at the thought. 'I wanted to be sitting with you.' I immediately wished I could take that back; it just made me sound needy.

'Oh.'

'But you were just with those boys,' I continued, despite a voice inside my head screaming at me to shut up. 'And when you were speaking to Scott, I thought yay because you don't have a boyfriend, but then I thought oh no because you don't want to hang around with me.' I knew I was speaking quite matter-of-factly, but I also knew I sounded desperate.

'I didn't mean to upset you. I just… something really embarrassing happened to me with a girl at a party once, and I didn't want that to happen again. That's why I was hanging around with boys I didn't know.'

We had nearly reached our houses and my ability to be tactful was nowhere to be found. 'What happened?'

Alana inhaled. 'It's not important.' Before I could ask again, she continued. 'Thank you for tonight, Emily, and I'm sorry it didn't go according to plan. I shouldn't have agreed to us going.'

'You don't need to apologise.'

Alana gave me a rueful smile. 'I want to. I've been trying to work on my impulsiveness.' She placed a hand on my side, before letting it fall again. 'I'm sorry for putting you in that situation.'

I couldn't find the words to explain that I was sorry too, so the two of us stood in silence at the bottom of my driveway until Alana gave me a hug to say goodbye. As she did so, I felt my lips graze her cheek, just like hers had done to mine in the photo booth. The action made me freeze as I tried to work out whether it was purposeful or not, mentally vowing to never drink alcohol again.

'Thanks for going with me.' My voice was muffled by her hair, and she laughed as she pulled away and started to walk towards her own house.

'Anytime.'

That night, it took me hours to fall asleep; every time I closed my eyes, I saw images of Scott trying to touch Alana. I also saw pictures of me wanting to help but being paralysed by, not quite fear, but anger. As I began to feel myself sobering up more, I realised just how messed up the party had been; Alana had been assaulted in a room full of people who hadn't stopped it happening. And I'd been one of those people. I lay awake for a while, concentrating on patterns I could see inside my eyelids, and I hoped Alana would forgive me in the morning. Eventually, I slept out of sheer exhaustion.

I had never felt as conscious during a dream as I did that night; it was as if I was completely in control of what was happening and the whole time I was aware it wasn't real. The sun was rising, and I was walking along a deserted beach, when suddenly I could hear someone running up behind me. Before I had the chance to turn, I heard laughter and felt a weight on my back that pulled me down to the sand. Alana was then sitting up next to me, her hair wild and her ears free of her hearing aids. I tried to sign to her but found I couldn't remember how to. She looked down at my hands.

'I have the implants now, Emily; you don't need to sign for me anymore.' Alana was shaking her head and her eyes were wide. I felt honoured at the fact I could see myself in them.

'You can hear?'

'I can. Now everything's perfect.' She looked at the waves as I looked at her, and I could hear the sound she loved so much. It was rhythmic and beautiful, and I was getting lost in it. So lost that I forgot I was in a dream, and I reached over to cup the side of Alana's face. She turned to me once again, almost as if she knew what I wanted to do before I did, and we leaned in together at the same time. My lips touched hers just as I heard a low vibrating noise that started to increase in volume.

My eyes snapped open and I was back in my room, my phone lit up beside me. It read '*Low battery. Please charge now*' right below the obnoxiously bright clock reading 3am.

'Oh.' I rubbed the sleep out of my eyes and grasped at the wires beside my bed before I felt the right one. After switching its sound off, I plugged my phone in. 'Oh.'

In the back of my mind, I was somewhat aware of my pounding headache, but all I could think about was my dream. I tried to figure out why I was dreaming about Alana and, more importantly, why I was dreaming about kissing Alana. I wondered if I still had alcohol in my system. Eager to have the internet rule out any possible causes, I turned the brightness down on my phone and decided to search for some answers.

'I had a dream about kissing a girl.' That brought up a load of results describing the symbolism of kissing (passion and loyalty, apparently). It also suggested I had done something in my dream that I was too scared to do in real life, but that didn't make sense; aside from when we were saying goodbye after the party, I had never thought about kissing Alana: not even after the photo booth incident. I'd never actually thought about kissing any girl, ever. When I was younger, I'd imagined marrying pop stars and actors from films I liked (even certain cartoon princes), but never girls. I made my question more specific to me.

'I dreamt about kissing my same-sex friend.' I almost didn't click the search button; I wanted to remain ignorant for a little while longer. Whilst part of me knew I could blame my dream on the alcohol I'd ingested, another part of me knew I didn't hate the idea of the dream being reality; I didn't hate the idea of really kissing Alana, and I certainly didn't hate the idea of lying on a beach with her. I brushed my thumbnail against the pad of my finger, wondering what was wrong with me; Alana was my first real friend and I was possibly ruining our relationship by dreaming about kissing her. I tried to put the phone down and go back to sleep, but I couldn't; I needed to find an answer.

The webpages that showed up when I searched my sentence were of varying quality; some were heartfelt blog posts in which gay teenagers recounted their sexual awakening, others were posts from a question and answer forum with less than helpful answers. The gems included such comments as 'sounds like ur gay' and 'bicurious much?'.

As I lay in bed, I wondered if that's what I was. If I was just open to the idea of a relationship with a girl, rather than genuinely interested in pursuing one, or whether I just felt so close to Alana that I could picture us dating. I knew I was more likely to be 'bicurious' than I was to be gay; I liked boys. Even though my feelings for James had been less than intense, I had been attracted to him and had had crushes on other guys. That led to my next search: 'Am I bisexual?'. The fact that I was questioning my sexuality thanks to a girl I had known for a few days didn't even cross my mind. Nor did the fact that, if you have to search whether or not you're straight, you're probably not.

That last search presented me with a list of tests, scales, flow charts and even quizzes to help me identify myself, and I couldn't believe how many other people had asked the same question. I had always thought that people just knew who they were: that people were born fully aware of themselves and who they had the capacity to love. I didn't realise there were *other* eighteen-year-olds like me, and people who were even younger and older, who turned to the internet to try and find out who they were. On the one hand, I was relieved to know I wasn't alone. On the other, I was distraught at the thought that thousands of other people had felt as confused and lost as I did that morning.

The more I read, the more I wondered what would have happened if I'd never met Alana; would I have gone through my whole life thinking I was straight?

Would I have fallen for some other girl somewhere along the line? I didn't understand how a virtual stranger could cause me to rethink my whole sense of self, and I wondered if my brain was just trying everything it could think of to be less predictable.

As I debated the issue, my eyes began to close of their own accord and I felt my phone slip from my fingers as I fell asleep.

Chapter 7

As I'd forgotten to close my curtains, the sun woke me up a mere few hours after I had managed to go back to sleep. My head was still hurting and I could barely walk in a straight line, but I somehow made it downstairs. As if by magic, there was a glass of water and a box of paracetamol on the kitchen counter.

'Good morning, Emily.' I winced as my dad spoke, and brought my hand up to my forehead as if it would help ease the ache. 'How are you enjoying the horrors?'

'I can't say that I'm enjoying anything right now,' I said, before swallowing a gulp of water and two tablets. 'But thanks for the painkillers.'

'No problem. You do know that it's nearly eleven though, don't you?' He was putting trays in the oven as he spoke, and the noise he was making resembled that of a large, not particularly tuneful, brass band.

'Yeah, that's fine. Bye, Dad.' I walked back upstairs, my eyes only half-open so I didn't have to cope with too much light. I tried to figure out what possessed people to drink constantly when that feeling was the aftermath.

When I got back to my room, I looked straight through into Alana's, but she didn't seem to be there. Figuring that I didn't want to sleep when I knew she was up and about, I bypassed my bed and sat in front of my laptop. My headache was easing slightly but I still turned the screen brightness down as much as possible.

I went into my favourite webpages, then used the search tool on *learnbslforlife* to type 'translation for party'. Even though I wanted to discuss almost anything else with Alana, I figured that learning appropriate signs to describe the night before might be a good idea. The sign involved making a fist with each hand and holding out each thumb and little finger. I then had to move them around either side of my head. I also went on to learn 'alcohol' (it was similar to 'drink', but involved moving a pretend cup in circles near my mouth rather than pretending to drink it). Knowing that I would want to use it, I learnt 'sorry' too, and found that it was pretty simple; I just had rub circles on my chest with my fist. Alana still hadn't appeared in her window.

After waiting for a few minutes, I decided to go to her house and apologise in person for the disaster that was the night before. I had a quick shower and got dressed before heading over.

Linda was walking down the driveway when I got there, wearing her work uniform and texting on her phone.

'Hey Mrs Wilson! Is Alana in?'

'Emmy! Hi. She's not, actually.' She looked back at her house, then narrowed her eyes at me. 'She didn't tell you? She's at the doctor's.'

She hadn't told me, I thought. Or maybe she had. I wondered if maybe she had told me the night before, and I had just been too drunk to acknowledge what she was saying.

'Is she okay?'

'Yeah, she's fine.' Mrs Wilson carried on moving and I changed direction to walk beside her. 'I'm sure she'll tell you all about it later, but I really have to go, Emmy. I'm sorry.' She bustled off down the road, her fingers once again tapping at her phone screen.

I walked back to my house and retrieved my own phone from my bedroom floor to see if Alana had in fact texted me to let me know where she was going. She hadn't.

I wondered if maybe she suspected that I was attracted to her, and if that was why she didn't tell me. Then I thought how ridiculous that idea was; I barely had reason to think that, let alone her.

'Where did you just go?' Although it seemed a lot less intrusive than it had done earlier, my dad's voice once again made me jump. 'Oops, sorry.'

I stood up with my phone and joined him by my door. 'I went to see Alana, but she's gone out.'

He nodded. 'Well, your mum's still asleep so I've just been trying to decide what board game we're playing tonight. Do you have a preference?'

We started to walk through the hall and down the stairs together.

'We haven't played Catch a Cat in a while.'

Catch A Cat was a game of our own creation. It involved tiny plastic tigers, jelly beans and a deck of cards.

My dad started to laugh. 'That's because *your mum* threatened to burn the house down last time we tried to.'

I followed him into the kitchen. 'My mum? She was your wife first.'

Dad took a croissant-covered tray out of the oven and placed it on the island. We sat down opposite each other as he passed one to me. 'That's very true. Love makes us blind to many things.'

I could feel myself getting hotter at the use of… that word, and I took a bite out of the croissant. Unfortunately, I didn't realise how warm it was going to be. Instinctively, I spat the mouthful onto the counter.

'The croissants are hot,' I said hoarsely, picking up my drink from earlier and chugging it. My dad handed me a cloth.

'I think they usually are after being in the oven.' I stuck my tongue out at him and sat back down, cleaning the bits of half-chewed food. 'So, where is Alana?'

'She's at the doctor's.' I picked up the rest of my breakfast and blew on it. 'I don't know why.' After watching my dad have a bite of his own croissant with no difficulty, I tried another, smaller one of mine.

'Why don't you invite her over later? We have a pizza you can cook.'

That seemed like a good idea; I could see Alana and check that she was okay, and maybe check that I hadn't done anything I'd forgotten about the night before. More than anything, I could simply see her again.

I signed 'thank you', my mouth once again full of pastry.

'And that reminds me.' My dad clasped his hands together on the table. 'Emily, do you think you could teach me some sign language?'

'What?' Crumbs sprayed out of my mouth in every direction. I was not a clean eater that morning.

'You're making a complete haymes of that,' he said, before retrieving some surface wipes and handing them to me. 'I'm saying that I want to be able to speak to Alana properly.'

'Well, I'd love to teach you some,' I said, after swallowing what was in my mouth 'Shall we begin with introductions? I mean, she already knows you, but it's a start.'

'Okay, thank you.'

So, in the same way that he taught me English and bits of Gaelic, I taught my dad how to sign. Within minutes, he'd learnt the alphabet and various greetings. He was fingerspelling his name when my mum walked in, rubbing her eyes with the backs of her hands.

'Why are you both up so early?' she murmured, switching on the coffee machine. 'It's the weekend; we should still be sleeping.'

As we both knew better than to reply before she'd had her fix of caffeine, my dad and I started to sign again, this time without speaking at the same time.

'D- O- D- E-A -F -P -E- O- P-L E- S- W- E- A- R?' he spelt out. I grinned, imagining how proud Alana would be in that moment.

'Y- E- S.' I demonstrated some of the signs that Alana had shown me, spelling out what each one was afterwards. Just as my dad was repeating 'bitch', my mum sat with us.

'Mark, are you signing?'

He tried to bite back a smile. 'I am; Emily is teaching me how to speak to Alana.'

'You are, Emily?'

'Yeah. I kind of feel sorry for her as the only person she can really talk to is her mum.' I smiled innocently.

'Is that so? In that case, maybe I should learn to sign too.' My mum took her hands off from the sides of her mug and repeated the sign for 'bitch'. I cleared my throat as she did so, trying desperately not to laugh or look surprised. 'What does this mean?'

I looked to my dad for some assistance, but he had turned away, his shoulders moving up and down and his face covered by his hand.

'We'll get to that later, Mum,' I said gently, before placing the last piece of my croissant into my mouth.

My mum nodded slowly. 'Oh, okay.'

'I can teach you what we've just done though!' I tried to say, my teeth coated in gooey pastry. 'Like the alphabet.'

Within fifteen minutes, she too could recite the alphabet and introduce herself. I hoped that it would help make Alana feel more at home around us.

'Is she coming over today?' my mum asked after she had signed 'Hello Alana, my name is Sarah'.

'I told Emily that she's more than welcome to invite her,' said my dad. He was fingerspelling his name over and over again as he spoke, almost as if he was trying to work out how quickly he could do it.

'I'll message her now,' I said, quietly relieved that I had a reason to message her first. I unlocked my phone and saw that all of my tabs from earlier on were still open.

'What have you been reading?' my mum asked, peering over my shoulder. I minimised the windows.

'Just some question and answer forums,' I said truthfully, before sending a message to Alana and locking my phone again. I wondered what my parents would do if I told them I didn't think I was straight. I was pretty sure they'd be cool with it; neither of them seemed homophobic, but I wasn't ready to bring it up. Not when I wasn't even sure if I wasn't straight; I didn't know if I could trust a dream. Alana responded almost immediately.

Thanks! I'd love to come over. I can be there in ten minutes?

Perfect!

I closed the messaging window and put my phone down on the counter.

'Alana says she'll be here in ten minutes; she must have already left the doctor's.'

My mum opened her mouth as if to ask a question, but my dad shushed her.

'Do you want to put some food in now then?' he asked. 'It will be ready for lunchtime if you do.'

'Yeah, I will.'

'And I'm going for a shower,' he said, standing up and clearing the counter as I made my way over to the freezer.

'I might join you,' said my mum, winking. I gagged over the pizza as I put it in the oven.

'That's horrific. Please never say anything like that again.'

After my parents left me and I had waited for what felt like an hour, I heard somebody at the door. Before I could feel excited, however, I remembered just what had happened the night before. I remembered throwing up in front of a girl I later dreamed of kissing: a girl who was far too cool to be hanging around with me anyway. I remembered watching her be assaulted and being unable to make myself intervene. I prepared myself for the worst; I knew Alana could have agreed to come over just to say she didn't want to see me again.

'Emily? Your front door was open.' She was suddenly standing in front of me, a black beret resting on top of her curls and matching her black mid-length dress and heels.

'Alana. Hey.' What a great reply that was.

'Hey.' She took her backpack off her shoulder and placed it on the floor before taking her phone out. 'Are you okay?'

'Yes! Why wouldn't I be?' As I looked at her, I tried to imagine us kissing. I tried to decide whether or not that seemed like a fun idea when I was sober.

'Because of how much you drank last night…' Alana trailed off and I realised I had been gradually getting closer to her. I skirted to the side as if I had meant to lead her to the living room. 'I figured you might be a little hungover.'

'I'm okay.' I flicked the television on and sat on the couch. Alana sat beside me and I could smell her perfume; it was a mix of vanilla and possibly strawberries. Maybe cherries. I realised that thinking about kissing her was a bad plan. No, a terrible plan.

'I'm glad.' The room went quiet.

'So how did your appointment go?' I asked eventually. As soon as the words left my mouth, I clamped my lips together to try and stop myself from asking anything more. Anything like *why didn't you ask me to go with you?*

'It was good, thank you.' She looked over at the television screen and I turned the subtitles on for her, mortified that I hadn't thought to before. 'But the doctor wants to wait a while before we move ahead with the implants.'

'That's okay, though. Right?'

Alana turned back to me. 'Yeah.' She smiled a little and moved ever so slightly closer. 'I've been thinking about everything I'm going to do when I have them, and I think the first thing I'd want to do is go to the beach.'

I tried to respond to her, but ending up choking on nothing in particular as images of me kissing her in front of the sea started playing in my mind. Alana looked around the room for a second, before she started to pat me on the back. Eventually, I stopped coughing.

'Of course, so you can hear the sea again,' I said, almost normally, when I was more composed.

'Yeah. I miss it.' A film began to play on the TV. It was black and white and seemingly French, but I didn't want to turn it over on the off chance Alana wanted to watch it. Plus, I figured that a foreign language film might be a good middle ground for the two of us; Alana needed subtitles because she had trouble hearing the dialogue, and I needed them because I couldn't understand it. Although I knew I could never imagine Alana's difficulties, I almost managed to kid myself that we were in a similar situation. It was like it made me feel closer to her.

'Is there anything else that you'd want to do after the operation?' I asked, grateful that I managed to do so in my regular voice.

'I've never been to a concert, so I think I'd like to experience one.'

'I've never been to one either,' I confessed. I thought back to how everyone else in my school used to spend hundreds of pounds on tickets to see people that I'd never heard of. 'I think I'd like to, though, but I don't really listen to music.'

Alana widened her eyes at the second part of my statement. 'Then we shall go to one together,' she announced. *Together*. I liked the sound of that. 'As soon as I have my implants.'

'That sounds perfect.' In reality, the thought of being with Alana in a sweaty, crowded music venue nearly made me choke again, but I managed to settle for clearing my throat. 'How is your hearing today?'

'It's been worse before. And better. It just kind of feels like I'm still at the party and trying to hear you over the music.'

'Oh. I'm sorry.'

'No, it's not actually because of the party or anything! Don't worry. I just have good days and bad days.'

'I see.' I watched the film for a few seconds as I willed myself to say something. *Anything*. 'I had a dream about you last night.' I should have willed myself to say anything but that.

'You did?' Alana waggled her eyebrows at me, drawing my attention to the beautiful eyes underneath. They really seemed to get greener every time I saw her. 'Should we be having this conversation so early in the day? I think that we should keep things PG until dinnertime.'

'It wasn't like that!' It was exactly like that. 'In it, you just. You could hear.'

'Really?'

'Yeah. It was weird though; I kind of missed signing with you.'

'But don't you find it really tiring?' I noticed that Alana's shoulders were partially slumped, and she spoke as if she felt like she knew, and dreaded, the answer. 'I mean, it's a lot of effort.'

'Not at all,' I said honestly, signing enthusiastically as if to prove my point. 'Sign language is beautiful, and I really love learning it.'

'Do you actually mean that? I've always thought that me losing my hearing was just a huge burden on everyone.' Alana didn't look at me as she spoke, her voice gradually getting quieter. It was as if the joking girl from mere seconds ago had been replaced with a smaller, more insecure replica.

'I mean it. And you could never be a burden.' I didn't understand how she could find what I was saying so hard to believe; how she didn't know just how much effort she was worth. Maybe it was because she was my first proper friend, maybe it was because I was still confused about the previous night, but I knew that I never wanted her to feel like she was any trouble.

'I guess BSL does have its benefits,' she said. 'I mean, you can talk underwater or in the cinema or at awful house parties where the music is far too loud.'

'Are all parties as bad as that one was?'

'Oh, definitely.' She laughed dryly. 'Sometimes you get lucky and actually enjoy yourself for the first hour or two, but yeah they tend to be that bad.'

Just then, Alana's phone started to vibrate loudly. She took it off her leg and swiped the screen, but it went black before it could be unlocked.

'What was that?'

'Oh, my mum was trying to video call me.' She frowned, before dropping her mobile down on the couch. 'But my phone just died.'

'You can borrow mine if you want.' I took it out of my pocket and handed it over. 'Do you know her number?'

'Yeah, I do. Thank you, Emily.' As Alana went to unlock it, I remembered what I had been searching on my phone that morning. I remembered that the tabs were still open because I'd only minimised them, and that my recent internet searches always appeared on the home screen.

'Wait!' I lunged forward to grab it, and Alana released it immediately.

'What? What did I do?' I looked from her face to the phone and back to her face, wondering just how crazy I looked.

'You didn't do anything.' I tried desperately to think of something that could justify me literally jumping on top of her. 'Just. My phone is really hard to navigate and I forgot. I'll type in your mum's number for you if you tell me what it is.'

'Okay. Thanks,' Alana replied slowly, and I could have sworn that she was leaning away from me.

I could feel my face getting hotter as Alana recited Mrs Wilson's mobile number and, when I handed her the phone, I forced myself to consider the possibility of just being honest about my dream. I figured that maybe she'd tell me every girl thinks about kissing other girls when they've been drinking, or maybe that dreams really don't mean anything. For a split second, I let myself think that maybe she would tell me that she'd had a similar dream. That, even though we'd only met recently, she had thought about kissing me too, and not just on the cheek, and that our jokes were really just our way of flirting with each other.

It wasn't until I watched how effortlessly she signed to Mrs Wilson, and how often she smiled when she mouthed her words, that I realised how much I wanted that latter thought to be accurate. I realised that, even though I barely knew her, I wanted her to want to kiss me. It occurred to me that even though my dream was the result of intoxication, I genuinely liked the thought of being with Alana like that; I wanted to kiss her in real life too.

That's when I knew that I couldn't be honest about my dream; I knew Alana would be disgusted and would never want to see me again, and that she'd probably think of me as some crazy lesbian stalker. I couldn't bear that thought; I knew I wanted Alana however I could have her, and that silently pining after her but remaining friends was a million times better than voicing my new feelings and being pushed away.

As she ended her video call, I accepted that how I felt towards her wasn't the same way I should have felt towards a new friend. I toyed with the fact that I wanted to be with her for as long as possible, in a way that I knew meant I'd been wrong about my identity for the last eighteen years. It suddenly seemed even more likely that I was bisexual.

If She Favours You

'Hey, thanks again,' Alana said, bringing me out of my daydream. I took the phone off her, somewhat reeling from what I'd let myself discover. 'Are you alright? Your mum sent a text, but I can reply to it if you want.'

'She what?' I looked down to see the unopened message.

Planning an online shop. Is there anything you still need for your uni room? X

I hesitated before responding; the reminder that I was due to move away at the end of summer was enough to make me freeze for a moment.

I don't think so x

Okay! I would have come down and asked but your dad and I are still in our towels x

Ew. That was not an image I needed in my brain.

'Is everything okay?' Alana was fiddling with her hair like she'd done the day we met.

I made myself smile. 'Everything's fine. My mum just can't go more than a few hours without offering to buy stuff for my university room. She doesn't understand that stereotypical Art students thrive on owning the bare minimum.'

Alana's head snapped up as she dropped the section of hair. 'You're moving out for university?' It sounded more like a statement than a question, but Alana was looking at me expectantly.

'Well, yeah. It's not too far away, though.' Alana didn't respond so I looked back at the film. After no more than two minutes, I reached for the remote and turned off the television, unable to bear not hearing her voice. 'Are you moving away for university?'

'No. I don't actually know what I'm doing, but I'm not going to uni.'

'But why not?' First it was James, then it was Alana. I wondered if I would be as calm as them if I didn't have a solid plan for the next few years, then realised that I knew I wouldn't be.

Alana pointed at her hearing aids. 'I don't think that I would cope well with the university lifestyle.'

'Because of your hearing?' She didn't react. 'Alana, I don't think you should let that stop you from doing something you want to do. What course would you have chosen?'

'You mean if it was taught in sign language and I wouldn't feel constantly alienated?' I nodded, ignoring her sharp tone. 'I would've picked primary teaching.'

'You want to be a teacher?' I hadn't expected any particular answer from Alana, yet I was still surprised to hear that one.

'I did. Not anymore.'

'What changed?'

'Em, you know exactly what changed.' Although the fact that Alana had given me a nickname made me want to leave the room and squeal like a six-year-old, I tried to stay calm. 'I'm going deaf; I can't be a teacher.'

I clenched both of my fists together in front of myself, before quickly splaying out my fingers, my palms facing downwards.

'Did you just *bullshit* me?' The pitch of Alana's voice was surprisingly high all of a sudden.

I signed 'yes' before repeating the previous action.

'It is not bullshit, okay? I can't teach a class of students if I can't even hear them.'

'Teach Deaf kids,' I signed without speaking, matching Alana's hard stare with one of my own. 'Teach hearing kids sign language. You can still teach.'

'And what if I don't want to?' Her voice was now loud as well as high, and I was horrified at the thought that I'd actually made her angry. 'What if I want to teach kids maths and history? And what if I want to teach kids who aren't Deaf because I want to feel normal again?' Her voice was breaking, and I could feel myself trembling at seeing her upset.

'Being hard of hearing doesn't mean that you're not normal,' I told her as firmly as I could, signing the words that I knew. 'And why the hell would you want to be normal anyway? You're extraordinary. And that's far better.' Shit. I did not mean to say all of that. Shit. That was definitely not heterosexual behaviour.

'Emily, you barely know me,' Alana said after a pause, no longer shouting. 'You can't call me that. Besides, I'm fine with the thought of finding a new career path.'

'But you can teach if you want to,' I insisted, beyond relieved that Alana hadn't explicitly questioned my choice of words. 'You could even have a teaching assistant to work as a translator for the kids when they're talking to you.'

'What will it take to get you to drop this?'

Honestly? Nothing more than you asking me to. I thanked God for the fact that I managed to refrain from saying that aloud.

'You realising exactly what you're capable of.' I didn't want to upset Alana further, but I also didn't want to let the topic go completely. 'I mean, I met you and then two days later I went to a party. If you can make me be sociable, you can do anything.' Alana rolled her eyes but there was no malice in her expression. 'And I want you to know that you would flourish in university and as a teacher. I'm sure of it.'

'Thank you,' she signed after a minute. I tried to ignore how much she looked like she was blowing me a kiss; I needed to start thinking straight around her. Literally.

'So, did you hate that film too or was it just me?' I asked, trying to dispel the awkward tension that had settled. I felt myself relax Alana chuckled.

'Yeah, I hated it too.'

'Shall we see if the pizza's cooked?'

'I thought you'd never ask.' Alana jumped off the couch and, once again, held out her hand. I hesitated for a second, wondering if she'd be so willing to make physical contact with me if she knew I'd dreamed about her the way I did. Maybe I was just as bad as Scott had been at the party; he'd thought that he had a chance with Alana despite her disinterest too. Though, no: I knew that I didn't have a chance. I made myself take her hand and I could have sworn that it felt clammy. She let go once I had stood up. 'Do you have any ice cream?'

'We do.' I led her into the kitchen and took the pizza out of the oven. Its crust had become the perfect dark brown, almost black, colour. 'Why?'

'Because you can't have pizza without ice cream.'

I was just taking a pair of scissors out of the cutlery drawer when Alana's words sunk in. 'What?'

'Pizza and ice cream. Is that your freezer?' She pointed at the bottom half of the fridge and I nodded. She opened the door and pulled out an ice cream tub. 'It's quite literally the best thing since sliced bread.'

'But that sounds disgusting.' I put the tray down and began to cut the pizza into slices, trying to comprehend why anybody would mix hot savoury food with ice cream. 'And it's really weird.'

'Weird? You're the one cutting pizza with scissors!' Alana looked as surprised as I felt. 'Why don't you use a pizza cutter?'

'Why don't you eat pizza with pasta? Or anything that isn't ice cream?' I divided the pizza between two plates, shaking my head at the thought of mixing two completely different foods.

When Alana started to scoop some ice cream onto her pizza, I felt myself growing queasy.

'No. You're not actually doing that, are you?' She didn't respond, instead choosing to taint my pizza with vanilla ice cream too. I watched as it immediately started to melt. 'You did not...'

'Try it.' She grinned, handing me a spoon.

I could have said no; I could have scraped the ice cream off and salvaged my lunch, but I didn't. I couldn't. Not when Alana looked at me like she was trusting me with some huge secret. I cut off a piece of pizza with the edge of the spoon and mixed it with some ice cream, bracing myself for the disgusting taste.

'And?'

To my surprise, it wasn't bad. 'Okay, it is pretty good.' Though it pained me to admit it, there was something about the tomato sauce mixing with vanilla that was weirdly delicious.

'Pretty good? You are the first person I have ever trusted with this recipe and that's all you have to say about it?' Alana took my plate from me and carried it, along with her own, to the living room. 'You don't deserve the miracle that is ice cream on pizza.'

'Alana!' I protested, turning the oven off and following her out. 'I'm hungry!'

She was sitting on the sofa again, a plate in each hand. 'Do you still think that it's disgusting?'

'Kind of.' She raised an eyebrow at me and I sat down beside her, still unfamiliar with how the whole process of teasing a friend (yes, *friend*, that was all she would ever be) was meant to go. I went to grab my plate, but she held it upwards so I couldn't reach it. 'But it's still nice! It shouldn't be, but it is.' Alana lowered the plate ever so slightly.

'You still don't seem to fully appreciate it,' she said, before exhaling loudly as if she was debating whether or not to hand me my lunch back. 'But it's a start.' As she gave it to me, I saw that nearly all the ice cream had melted. It smelt incredible.

'Okay, well I think you're a genius then.' I ate another scoop and she did the same. 'And just because something is theoretically gross, that doesn't mean it tastes that way.'

'That's more like it.'

'Are you having ice cream on pizza?' My mum's voice and sudden presence in the doorway made me jump.

'Yeah,' I replied, just as my dad appeared beside her. 'It's actually quite nice.'

'That's definitely an understatement,' said Alana, addressing my parents. She held out her spoon to them. 'Would you like to try it?' Their scrunched-up noses and wide eyes were enough of an answer, so Alana just nodded and gave a small laugh. 'Thank you for having me by the way, Mr and Mrs Wilson.'

'It's our pleasure,' said my mum, smiling as she did so. I don't know if I'd ever seen someone smile as they spoke before, but I never wanted to again. 'And please, call me –' She looked down at her fingers as she spelt her name. 'S-A-R-A-H. Sarah.'

'And my name is Mark.' My dad signed his whole sentence. 'Hello Alana.'

I heard an 'Oh' from Alana and I froze. I wondered if I'd done the wrong thing by teaching my parents sign language when she obviously hoped to hear again. Despite being scared of how she was reacting, I turned to her. To my surprise, she was smiling.

'Thank you for learning that,' she said, translating it into sign language as she did so. She looked back at me. 'Did Emily teach you?'

My mum nodded exaggeratedly. 'She did.'

'Thank you,' Alana mouthed. Before I could respond and, as if they hadn't realised that I could still see them, my parents decided to kiss in the doorway. Alana must have noticed my horrified expression because she looked back over at them.

'Mum, Dad. Can you not, please?' My words did nothing to stop them.

'It's sweet,' said Alana, shaking her head at me. 'You know, that they're still in love even now.' I raised my eyebrow at her, having forgotten how romantic she had seemed when we first met. 'Love can change the world, Emily.'

Maybe she had a point there; love was changing my world. *No, not love.* I told myself. Nope. I couldn't love someone I hardly knew. Especially not when I didn't even know if I was gay; I decided that my feelings for Alana would probably pass in a few weeks. I kind of hoped that they wouldn't, though.

'Sweet is not the word I was thinking of,' I said, as my parents pulled away from each other. A second later, they wandered into the kitchen with their arms around each other's waists. I mimed being sick. 'So, now that we've been truly disgusted, what do you want to do?'

'Do you have a laptop? We could see what concerts are on this summer.'

'Yeah, it's in my room.' I led the way upstairs, ignoring the kissing noises coming from the kitchen, and it was only when Alana walked with me to my desk that I remembered what I'd been drawing.

'Is that –?' A huge canvas adorned with your face lying on my bedroom floor? Yep. 'Is that me?'

'Well, kind of, yeah.' That was one of my less intelligent answers. I tried to placate myself with the thought that, even though ruining Alana's surprise present would have been much more preferable to looking like a stalker, at least her picture didn't look at all sea-like in that moment. 'I just wanted to paint somebody new.' That was a half-truth at least.

'It's amazing.' She knelt in front of it and placed her bowl beside her. 'I had no idea that you could do this.' Alana looked up at the paintings decorating my walls. There were portraits of my parents and our old dog Jasper, as well as various landscapes. 'Did you do all of these? And the ones in your hall?'

'Yeah. I have a lot of free time.' I laughed nervously, wondering why she wasn't completely freaked out by my canvas. At least it was realistic enough that she wasn't offended.

'If you're this good now, I can't wait to see how good you are when you get back from university.' She stood back up, then sat on my bed with my laptop. I joined her and typed in my password.

'Well, thank you.'

Alana spoke again before I could overthink her compliments. 'Okay, now let's see who's performing this summer.' She started to search for concerts in our area. A list soon appeared, and on it was a bunch of singers that I'd never listened to. I watched as Alana scrolled through the names. 'Wait, that says Isadora Duncan!' Yeah, I had no idea either. She clicked on the link to the dates. 'And there are tickets left! That's definitely the concert we need to go to.'

'Sure.' I was willing to sit through anything, even the musical equivalent of nails down a chalkboard, if I could do so beside Alana. 'I mean, I really love her stuff.'

'It's a band.' She smiled, the corners of her eyes crinkling as she pointed at one of the pictures on the screen. It showed three women dressed in black, each with different coloured hair. The one in the middle was wearing a dress and her hair was bright blue; those either side of her wore leather jackets and jeans. One had purple hair, the other pink. 'And she's my favourite.' Her finger circled the one with the blue hair. 'Her name is Skye. She's dating Daisy: the one with the pink hair. The other one's called Megan and she's engaged to Daisy's brother.'

So, Alana's favourite band member happened to be dating a girl. That had to mean something, I hoped. At the very least, it had to mean she wasn't homophobic.

'They sound like a real-life soap opera.'

'Think modern day ABBA, but with rock music and leather.' We read the prices of the available tickets. 'Emily, this says we can get standing tickets right at the front for the same price as seated ones!'

'Yay?' I tried to work out if that was a good thing or not.

'I'll book them now; I have my card.' She took the cover off her phone, revealing a five-pound note and a debit card.

'Isn't that a bit hasty?' I asked, watching her type. 'I mean, what if –' I cut myself off just in time, wondering if the alcohol from the night before was still in my system; I didn't know why else I'd ever consider saying something that might hurt Alana's feelings.

'What if what? I don't get the implants?' she said, her nails still tapping on the keyboard.

'Well –'

'Well, then I'll only be able to partly hear them singing.' She smiled at me, her lips tightly pressed together, before continuing. 'I'll have the implants. I know it.' Alana tapped the enter key with a flourish.

'I'm sure you will.' I wasn't sure. Not at all. But I wanted Alana to have the implants because that's what she wanted. 'And I'm very excited to see Daisy? And Skye?'

'Don't forget Megan.' Alana switched my laptop off and put the lid down. 'And now the tickets are booked, so there's nothing stopping you from learning their whole discography.'

'Okay, thanks. I can pay you back.' I started to stand, so I could take my money box off the windowsill, but Alana put her hand on my leg.

'No, it's my treat.' She looked down at her hand at the same time I did, before yanking it away quickly. It was basically the non-verbal equivalent of *no homo*; she was definitely straight. I cleared my throat.

'Are you sure? I have some money.'

'I'm sure. You do need to listen to them, though; they sing some really great stuff.'

So that's what we did; Alana found a playlist of theirs on her phone, and I listened as she signed along with the music. The songs were alright, but she was incredible.

'How can you do that so quickly?' I asked, after she'd signed the entirety of a particularly fast song.

'Practice.' She rubbed the two sides of her hands together as she held them out facing the floor. Another song started to play, this one slower. 'I saw a girl doing signed covers online when I first found out I was going deaf. Watching her helped me learn loads of words.'

'You should do it at the concert,' I told her, ignoring the soft ballad playing in the background; it sounded like a love song, which was not what I need to hear. 'As we'll be standing at the front, they might even see you.'

'No. No I'm not doing that.' Alana shifted so she was sitting on her hands. 'It's not a party trick to help me get noticed.'

'That's not what I meant!' I really needed lessons in social interaction; I hadn't been this bad at having conversations since I first started dating James and was expected to converse with his friends. 'I just thought you might want to do it.'

'I know, sorry.' Her cheeks bloomed red. 'I didn't mean to sound so mean, I just don't want to set myself apart from people and draw attention to myself. Especially not by doing that.'

'I get it.' At least, I hoped I did. I never wanted Alana to feel like an outcast; I had been one my entire life and, while it didn't completely suck, it wasn't exactly ideal living.

'Thank you.'

Chapter 8

As the weeks went by, I learnt more and more about sign language. Alana taught me the grammatical rules of BSL, and I spent most of my free time watching vocabulary videos, not that I had much free time; she kept me busy and I loved her for it. Quite literally, as much as I tried to convince myself otherwise. I refrained from thinking about the *L word* for as long as I could, but, the more I saw her, the more I felt it.

She took me to the cinema one day, to watch a film full of explosions and fight scenes, because she said that none of the dialogue in it would be worth hearing anyway. That was when I learnt that signing was the perfect way to talk in a movie theatre.

Another day, we visited the local farm, and she joked that she might have been better off losing her sense of smell than her hearing. That was the day I learnt that nothing, not even three inches of mud, could stop her from wearing heels.

Most days, however, we stayed in Vellichor and signed to each other over cups of coffee. Those days, I learnt that I would spend the rest of my life with her if I had the chance.

'I still can't believe I'll be able to hear them live,' Alana said, pouring more sugar into her mug. We'd been talking about Isadora Duncan and their new single. Well. Alana had been. I'd been watching the way her hair shone in the light every time she moved her head. She'd stopped straightening it, and her curls were as bouncy as ever. They were always the first thing I noticed when we met up, followed by her eyes. 'Emily?'

'Yeah, me neither.' I tried to speak clearly as I signed; That week, I'd noticed that Alana had begun to pay more attention to my lips when I spoke, and I did all I could to make reading them easier for her. Especially since Vellichor had been getting a lot busier; even I had trouble hearing over kids laughing and cutlery being dropped. 'What part of that sentence is the best bit? The hearing bit or the live bit?'

'Both.' She beamed. It was two days before she was due to see the doctor about her implants again, and every discussion we had always circled back to it. 'I'm so excited about that, that I'm not even nervous about the surgery anymore.'

'Then, I guess you don't need me to sleep over tomorrow night?'

I'd offered to spend the night before her operation with her weeks ago, when I hadn't been certain about my feelings, and Alana had agreed immediately. The fact that she wouldn't have agreed if she'd known about my recurring beach dream, was one that I tried not to focus on.

'Of course I still need you to!'

I didn't know how I felt about that; I knew I should be happy that Alana wanted me to stay with her, but I also knew that the night would be torture. I didn't know how I was meant to sleep in the same room as someone I'd dreamt about kissing.

'Then I'll be there,' I signed. Despite my doubts, she was still Alana. And I'd have given her the world if she'd asked for it.

'Good! And I was wondering, do you want to go back to my house now?' she asked, after finishing her cup of coffee. 'You still haven't been in my room, have you?'

'No, I haven't. I'd love to see it.'

'Then let's go!' We left the money for our meals on the table and waved to Mrs Wilson and Mr Costas as we left. The streetlights began to flicker on, almost as if they were trying to light the way for us.

We didn't talk until we reached Alana's house, and I took a deep breath before following her inside and to her room.

'This is what it looks like on the other side of the window!' Alana exclaimed. She dropped her bag on the floor and gestured to her bed. 'We can sit.'

'Can we?'

Her duvet was almost completely covered in photographs and paper wallets. Alana pouted at me, before making two small spaces. 'I mean, now we can sit.'

I walked over as she sat down, my feet sinking into her carpet. It was black and covered with glittery silver specks that made it resemble the night sky.

'I like your pictures,' I signed, noticing how the wall above her bed was more colourful than those I could see through my window. She had stuck up cards adorned with song lyrics and book quotes, as well as mini film posters and photographs with herself and Mrs Wilson in. Our photo booth strip was up there too, as was as a small plastic wallet holding the Isadora Duncan tickets.

'Thank you.' Alana patted the other clear space on the bed and I perched on the edge. 'I thought my walls were looking a little too plain, so I did some decorating before I met you this morning.' She looked up to watch me respond.

'I can help?'

'I'd love that, thank you.' She pointed at the piles on the bed. 'Just set aside anything you particularly like.'

I nodded and picked up one of the wallets. It was surprisingly heavy.

The first picture I saw had been taken in front of a large, unlit fireplace. Alana was standing in the middle of a group of girls, all of whom were holding plastic cups and wearing black dresses. There were balloons and beer bottles on the floor, and the girls who weren't wearing high heels were barefoot. Every picture that followed was similar, although the dresses, the fireplaces and, occasionally, the people, changed. I realised why Alana had seemed so unfazed by James' party all those weeks ago.

'You had a lot of friends,' I signed, startled by how many people she seemed to know in comparison to me.

'Not really.' Alana spoke smoothly, picking up a pile of what looked like her baby pictures. 'There was a group consisting of three of us and we were friends, the others were just people who invited us to their parties.'

'So, you three were the popular girls?' I was uncomfortable aware that I was doing a terrible job of hiding my disbelief. It wasn't that Alana didn't seem like the type of person to be popular; she was beautiful and she spoke with the confidence of someone who had always been listened to, but it was that she had chosen to be friends with me that summer. Popular people didn't choose to hang around with me.

That just felt like another reason why I couldn't confess how I felt about her; we clearly weren't as similar as I had thought. I remembered my first meeting with Mrs Wilson, and suddenly her cryptic comments about Alana's old friends made sense, or at least some of them did.

'You could say that.' She began to arrange her pictures into some sort of timeline. I looked through more photos, all of which were pretty much the same, and realised that Alana's seemingly effortless coolness was probably a result of her being so favoured in school.

'Your hair is straight in all of these,' I noted after a while. It was beautiful in every picture, but something about its naturally curly state made Alana look much softer. I also realised that she wasn't wearing her hearing aids in any of the photos.

'The girls insisted it looked better like that, but I prefer it curly; I think I look more like me.' It was really hard to not audibly agree with her. 'Though straight hair was easier to tie up for practice, I guess.'

'Practice?'

'I was a cheerleader.'

A cheerleader. A *cheerleader*. Whatever I'd been thinking about before was replaced with an image of Alana in a cheerleading outfit. I imagined a few wisps of hair escaping her ponytail and framing her face. She had the right kind of smile for a performer; it was the type that grabbed your attention and made you smile too. And she definitely had the right figure for an athlete.

'Oh.' To try and stop thinking about her being on a cheer team, I carried on sifting through Alana's pictures. Soon enough, I found one that stood out from the rest; it was quite a bit smaller than the 6x4s I had been looking at, and it was much darker. It seemed to have been taken from one of the parties I'd already seen pictures from; I recognised Alana's dress and the sofa she was sitting on. I squinted a little and managed to make out the girl she was sitting next to, sitting very close to in fact. Their faces were touching. I then realised it was actually their mouths that were –

'What is that?' I hadn't heard Alana talk so sharply before and I dropped the picture in surprise. We watched it fall off the bed.

'It's just –' She wasn't even watching my hands.

Alana bent over and picked the photograph up off the floor. She looked down at it and closed her eyes for a few seconds. I didn't know what to do; I didn't even know how I felt. Part of me was extremely jealous of the girl in the photo, the other part was more hopeful than I ever thought I could be; maybe I actually had a chance with Alana. Maybe she liked girls too.

As difficult as it was, I tried to push my feelings away when she finally looked up again. 'Are you okay?'

'I'm fine,' she said, her voice breaking. I took her hand in mine and tried to tell her that she could trust me, that she could say whatever she wanted and I would always be there for her, but neither the words or the actions would come. 'Her name was Eve.' Her fingers curled around mine. 'She transferred to my school last year and we got really close. The others didn't want her to be part of our group; it was as if they thought that the more people we were nice to, the less popular we would be. But I loved being around her, and I was sure they would too.'

I tried to ignore the tears that had begun to fall down Alana's cheeks, but I could feel my own eyes watering too. She continued to talk, staring straight ahead without even blinking.

'I pushed for her to be one of us. I invited her to all the events that I organised, and I brought her along to the ones I didn't. We were never not together, and we grew really close. At least, I thought we did.'

'You don't have to tell me if you don't want to,' I signed, before placing my hand in hers again. I couldn't bring myself to speak; the sight of Alana, someone who had been so unbelievably strong despite everything she was going through, just breaking was too much.

'We were alone at a party near the end of the year,' she said, ignoring me. It was as if I wasn't even there. 'We had both been drinking very heavily, and she looked beautiful. I knew I loved her, and I really thought she loved me back, so I took a chance and I kissed her. I even thought that she kissed me back for a minute, but then we heard the noise of a picture printing.'

Alana looked down, her hair falling over her face but not hiding the fact that tears were still falling.

'It was a boy from our class with a polaroid camera. Michael. He threatened to out us to the whole school. Eve managed to play the kiss off as us just being drunk and I got the photo from him, but she never spoke to me again. Our friends sensed the tension and, when I found out I was losing my hearing, I think they decided I wasn't worth the trouble. They replaced me with the girl I loved, and I never even got the chance to tell her how I felt.'

'Maybe she knew,' I said loudly, compensating for the fact that Alana wasn't looking at my lips. She scoffed before yanking her fingers from mine and folding her arms.

'That would just make it worse, wouldn't it?' She finally looked back up at me, her expression the exact opposite of the confident, carefree one she had in all of her pictures. 'That would suggest that she knew she could have had my love and she just didn't want it.'

I really didn't know what to say; I had never been any good at pep talks and my lack of a social life had meant that I never needed to be. However, for Alana, I willed myself to think of something.

'Then, she was an idiot,' I said finally, signing it a second later. I then realised how close I was to admitting my feelings, and I forced myself to keep my mouth shut for a few minutes; just because Alana had liked a girl in the past, it didn't mean that she could ever like me. 'So, you're not…?'

I wasn't even sure what exactly I wanted to ask; some part of me really did want to weigh up whether or not I had a chance with Alana, but I knew I was selfish to be thinking about myself. I reminded myself that the fact I loved her didn't give me the right to make the moment about my feelings instead of hers.

'I'm gay,' she said, her voice having returned to the unwavering tone I'd become used to that summer. The voice fit for a former popular girl. 'Deep down, I'd always known I was, but I'd never truly loved anyone until Eve.'

'Does your mum know?' Though I was trying to distract Alana from her past, I also wanted to hear about her journey. I had never met any openly gay people before and, even though I knew I wasn't a lesbian, I knew I could learn from her.

'Yeah, she was great when I told her.' Alana started to dry her eyes, and I did the same whilst she wasn't looking. 'I told her and my dad at the same time, soon after that party.' I sat up straighter; this was the first time she'd mentioned her father to me.

'He was less great. He moved out a week later to be with some woman he was having an affair with. My mum insisted I'd had nothing to do with it, but, you know.'

'Oh, Alana.' I couldn't believe her own dad had willingly walked away from her; I couldn't believe she'd had friends who chose someone else over her, and I couldn't believe that she had kissed someone who responded by leaving. I especially couldn't believe that other people didn't see her the way I did.

Alana just pointed at herself, then gave me a thumbs up.

'You're not fine,' I replied. I wondered if there was anything I could say or do to help her.

She gave me a sombre smile. 'I guess I'm not. I really thought I was, though. When my mum first suggested moving, I was thrilled at the thought of starting again; I was going to go back to being the girl who always falls in love.'

'And how do you think that's going?' I was almost afraid of the answer.

'Up until now, it's been going well; I met you, I've had an amazing summer, and I have a huge opportunity with these implants.'

'So, what's the problem?'

She looked down at the picture in her hand. 'I can't just forget them. Not Eve, not my dad. I pushed them away.' Her voice started to waver as she continued. 'I haven't let myself think about them for so long, but it's my fault that they hate me.'

'Never say that,' I signed, slightly more aggressively than I meant to. 'Don't blame yourself for their –' I fingerspelt 'intolerance.'

She didn't reply for a minute, but then: 'You don't hate me.' The surprise I heard in her voice as she let that fact sink in was heart-breaking. 'Eve and my dad both looked at me like I completely disgusted them. You haven't even inched away from me.'

'I could never hate you.' I wanted more than anything to explain exactly why that was, but I settled for squeezing her hand before continuing to sign. 'So, when you said about being scared to love someone?' She nodded and I resisted the urge to sigh. 'You know, Eve was stupid not to love you back.'

'She was actually really clever.' Alana's lips twitched as I released an exaggerated sigh.

'Well, so are you. You're clever enough to not care about what they think.'

'You're right; I moved on from them once and I'm sure I can do it again.' She must have noticed my unconvinced expression. 'It's fine, really. I'll just file this away as another one of my sad stories.'

'Just because you have sad stories, it doesn't mean you are one.' I knew that Charlie Kelmeckis would have been proud of me for saying that. 'And you don't need your dad or Eve.'

'But at the time, losing her actually hurt more than finding out I was losing my hearing.' She laughed humourlessly. 'I loved love so much, that I really thought it was worth more than a fundamental part of me.'

'What do you think now?'

'I think that to always fall in love is only sometimes the best way forward. And, as cliché as it sounds, I think I need to fall in love with myself before I can do so with someone else.'

'And do you think you have? Fallen in love with yourself, I mean.' I wanted her to say yes. It wasn't even just for me, as much as I wanted us to be together; I knew I'd gladly sacrifice her loving me if it meant that she loved herself.

'I think I'm getting there.'

'I can help you.' I thought I'd said the wrong thing then; Alana fell silent and gently stroked the edges of the picture of her and Eve. I watched her wordlessly.

'I could never bring myself to destroy this photo,' she said eventually, her eyes half-closed. I figured that she hadn't heard what I'd just said, which was probably for the best. I was about to tell her that she didn't need to destroy the picture, when she suddenly tore it right down the middle. Then again, and then again, until the pieces were too small to be recognisable. 'But now,' she continued, in a tone that could have been resentful but that simply wasn't, 'here lie the remnants of a relationship, in which Alana Wilson,' she paused and started to smile a little, 'in which Alana Wilson, to quote one great writer, loved not wisely but too well.'

I searched my mind to try and remember what that quote was from; it sounded vaguely familiar, but I couldn't for the life of me figure out why. I felt like it was one I'd heard, rather than one I'd read myself, which ruled out a lot of possibilities. Alana widened her eyes in mock amazement.

'Emily Davis, lover of classics, are you trying to tell me that you don't recognise an *Othello* quote when you hear one?'

'I'm not a huge fan of plays,' I signed hesitantly, grinning as her eyes crinkled. 'And anyway, what sort of popular girl annotates her copy of *Great Expectations* and casually quotes Shakespeare?' That latter part took a lot of fingerspelling, and Alana responded by grimacing.

'I prefer the term former popular girl.'

'That explains it, then.'

'And I read a lot because of Mr Foster, my English teacher.' Alana started to look through another stack of pictures. 'He was the only person in my school who knew sign language and he started to teach me it when he found out about my hearing. He used to sign different words and make me guess which book he was thinking of.'

'That's really sweet.'

'He was. I actually kind of miss him.' She pulled out one of the pictures and showed it to me. It depicted a class of students standing in two rows, with an elderly man sitting in the middle of the front one. Alana was standing right next to him, her hair poker straight and covering her ears.

'That's him?' I pointed at the whiskery face.

'Yeah. He was great.' She replaced the picture and looked up at me. 'Thank you for not hating me, by the way.'

'I really don't know why you think I'd do that.' I watched as her eyes flickered over to the torn-up bits of photograph paper. 'Because you're gay? Alana that would never change how I feel about you.'

Okay, so technically it did; it changed how I felt because it made me feel like I actually had a chance with her and, if I hadn't been so worried about her, it would have made me insanely happy. I wasn't about to say that, though.

'You're really something, Emily Davis.'

I tried not to show just how happy that statement made me.

'You're really something too.'

Chapter 9

When I got home, I sat on the floor by my window. After ensuring that I couldn't be seen from next door, I let the events of the day sink in. I let myself consider the possibility that Alana and I could ever be more than just friends, and I tried to come up with a coherent plan of action. Now that she had been honest with me, I wanted nothing more than to be honest too and for everything to work out well.

As my mum called me from downstairs to join in with board game night, I decided that I was going to tell her and my dad about my possible bisexuality. I realised that doing it during whatever game they'd chosen would guarantee that something else would take priority over my sexuality; both of my parents would be preoccupied with trying to win. I took a deep breath and went to the living room, placating myself with the truth that telling Alana was going to be a million times harder than telling them.

My parents were already teasing each other about who was going to win when I joined them. They were sitting on the floor around our old coffee table and playfully poking each other. I looked at their carefree expressions as my dad spread out the game board and passed my mum a bag of letter tiles. I tried to ignore the sinking feeling in my stomach; I knew I was incredibly lucky to have parents who probably wouldn't even care about what I was going to tell them, and I knew I had picked the right time to be honest about my feelings, but something stopped me from being able to speak.

Instead, after I had picked my tiles, I started the game with the word 'yacht'. 28 points. As I fished in the bag for more letters, I started to think about how this moment had the power to change my entire life; although I was confident that my mum and my dad wouldn't really think any less of me, they still weren't going to look at me in the same way. Plus, I knew that I needed to be honest with Alana once I had been honest with them.

'Emily, what's the matter with you?' Both of my parents were staring at me, and I looked down at the game board to see that two new words had been added.

'Sorry. I was just thinking.'

'Think faster,' my mum instructed. She consulted the score sheet in her hand. 'I have a game to win.'

'But I have something I want to tell you.' My leg twitched, despite me willing it not to.

'See if you can spell it out on the board.' She was seemingly oblivious to my nervousness. 'You could do with the points seeing as I'm going to beat you.'

'Mu-um,' I whined, wondering why I couldn't just *say it*; I wasn't ashamed, so I didn't know why it was so difficult.

'Is it really that bad?' my dad asked.

I exhaled slowly and shook my head before looking down at my letters. As luck would have it, I had picked up a 'G' before and I already had an 'A.' I placed them on the board on top of the 'Y' I had already put down.

'Fourteen points.' My mum wrote down my score and looked at her own letters. 'Now it's my turn.'

'Mum.' I tried to understand whether she'd just not read the word or whether she was trying to pretend she hadn't. I didn't really know what more I could do.

'A stór, are you trying to tell us that you're gay?' Dad spoke softly, leaning forward with his hands clasped together. He looked worried. Not disappointed, not surprised, but worried. I couldn't reply.

'Don't be ridiculous, Mark.' My mum placed the score sheet on the floor and spelt out her own word. 'Emily dated James for nearly a year; she's not gay.' It was only when I didn't respond for a while that she looked up at me. 'Right, Emily?'

'Well, I did go out with James.' My hands started to shake as well as my leg. 'And I liked him. But now I love someone. A girl. Alana, actually. And I know it's crazy, but I really think she could like me back. She might not do yet, but maybe one day.'

The sensation of saying that aloud was indescribable; I had known my feelings for a while but actually admitting them, and hearing myself doing so, that was unlike anything I'd ever experienced. I felt relieved; I felt free.

My mum was still frowning. 'So was James like...' She looked from me to my dad, then back to me. 'Was he your moustache?'

'My what?'

'Your moustache.' Her frown had cleared, and she looked at me with wide eyes. 'You know, your disguise so everybody thought you were straight.'

With that, my dad started laughing and I finally understood what she was trying to say.

'It's called a beard, Mum.' I thought back to her question. I'd definitely had feelings for James, but comparing how I had felt towards him to how I felt towards Alana was like comparing a match to an inferno. 'He wasn't one, though. I love boys and I love girls.'

My mum frowned, and I hoped against hope that she wasn't as disgusted as she looked. 'Isn't that just greedy?'

My heart sank. 'What do you mean?'

At the same time, my dad spoke. 'Sarah! It's called being bisexual, not being greedy.' I looked at him, my body finally feeling steady as I saw that there was really no horror on his face at all; aside from a slight frown that seemed more geared towards my mum, his expression was neutral.

'I'm not saying it's a bad thing,' said my mum. She replaced the tiles she had used, as if the conversation we were having was no more important than any other. 'Emily, you can like whoever you want to like.'

'We still love you no matter what,' added my dad.

'We do.' My mum smiled at me. 'Although I don't understand why you can't pick between boys or girls, and I don't really know how to accept something I don't understand.'

I tried to be grateful for the fact that she could have taken the news a lot more badly than she did, but honestly I just felt sick; she didn't need to understand it to accept it. I didn't understand half of the Gaelic my dad used, but I still accepted that he used it.

'You don't have to choose, sweetheart,' said my dad suddenly. 'After all, I never did.'

'What are you talking about?' I was feeling more and more overwhelmed the longer the conversation went on.

He looked down. 'I'm bisexual too.'

If it hadn't been for my mum suddenly beginning to wheeze, I would have sworn I'd imagined that confession. 'You are?' She spoke too bluntly for me to be glad that the attention wasn't on me anymore; I had a feeling that his confession wasn't going to be listened to as calmly as mine was.

'Why did you never tell us?' I asked, my head reeling as I tried to take in what I'd just heard. I could have pictured my coming out moment over and over again for years and still never have envisioned being in the scenario I was in.

'Because right now I love your mum, and that's all that matters.' My dad turned to Mum, as if he was about to kiss her on the cheek, but she lifted up her hand to stop him.

'You love me, but you've lied to me since we were eighteen?' Her tone was hurt more than anything, and I could feel my stomach turning violently; I had never seen her that upset before and it was all my fault. I couldn't believe I'd thought things were going well.

'I never lied to you, Sarah. I just never needed to tell you.'

'And you don't think I should have been the judge of that?' That was the first time I'd ever heard her raise her voice to my dad.

'Sarah, I –'

'No, Mark. You should have told me. It took our daughter coming out as a lesbian for you to be honest with me and you don't see that as a problem?'

'I'm not a lesbian.' I could hardly even whisper; my throat was unbearably dry and I was willing my mum to calm down.

'Sarah, please.'

'How many men have you been with?' I flinched at my mum's cutting tone. I then looked at the woman who wore aprons with puns on, and who bought my dad satin pyjamas for his birthday. I'd always known she wasn't the friendliest woman in the world, but she also wasn't the type to start an argument in the middle of a Scrabble game.

'That hardly matters! We've been together since we were in university and I have never once cheated on you; why would you care what happened before then?'

'How long have you known?' The board game had been forgotten, and my mum was edging away from my dad. 'How long?'

'Since before I met you.'

My mum's face had turned pale and I'd never hated myself as much as I did in that moment; in over twenty years of marriage, as far as I knew, my parents had never once fought like that. She put her head in her hands. 'I can't believe this.'

'I'm sorry, Mum.' I tried to put my arms around her in a desperate attempt to rectify the situation. 'I really didn't want to upset you.'

'You haven't, Emily.' She brushed me off and stood up. 'You have been honest and brave, and I love you. You're my daughter.' She turned on her heel and stormed out of the living room. She slammed the door behind her before running upstairs.

I looked at my dad, who was rubbing his neck and breathing heavily. 'Dad.'

'Don't worry about me, lovely.' His voice was no different than normal, but I could see him swallowing repeatedly. 'She'll come around.'

'I'm so sorry.' It took tears dripping down my cheeks for me to realise that I was crying, and I brushed them away fiercely; I had caused the argument, so I had no right to be upset.

'No, no.' My dad held his arms out to me and I sat on his lap, leaning into his embrace. 'I'm glad that you felt safe enough to tell us. I've never told your grandparents.' There was a moment of silence.

'Did you ever tell anyone?' My voice was hardly coherent due to the fact I was resting my head on his shoulder, but my dad tensed a little, so I knew he'd heard me.

'I told one person. His name was Stephen Hope. He was the only boy I ever dated, nearly a year before I met your mum. He was gay.'

'What was he like?' I was glad that my dad was wearing normal clothes for once so I wasn't wrecking one of his work suits with my tears and snot. As I'd calmed down slightly, I wanted to learn about him, about the stories he'd been too scared to tell, and I wanted to tell him I loved him no matter what, just like he'd told me. I wished that my mum wanted to do the same.

'He was handsome and charming, and all of the girls loved him; none of them knew, of course.' I got off my dad's lap and sat beside him so I could look into his eyes as he spoke. 'Stephen helped me find out who I was; in a world that told us you could be straight or you could be gay, he showed me that there were more options. Even though I wasn't honest publicly, I could be honest with him.'

'Where is he now?'

'He died whilst we were together.'

My mouth opened as I focused on my dad's bottom lip, suddenly unable to make eye contact. It quivered slightly as I spoke to him. 'What?'

My dad was looking at his hands as he scratched one fingernail with another. 'He killed himself during the last year of school. His parents found us together and they threw him out of their house. The police found him in a canal a week later.'

'Dad.' I looked at the man who had brought me up. The man who had bought me my first paintbrush, with the words 'dream big, darling' carved into the handle. The man who sent me texts from work to remind me that him and my mum loved me. I looked at him and my heart ached; if he'd never told my mum about his sexuality, there was no way he'd told her about Stephen. 'I'm so sorry.'

'His parents didn't even seem upset.' My dad's eyes were watering, and his nail was moving faster now. 'It was as if Stephen had done them a favour. They preferred having a dead son over having a gay one.'

I couldn't begin to imagine how my dad must have felt; how alone and miserable that must have made him. I always pictured his love life as being completely ideal, thanks to him finding my mum and then staying with her for so long. I couldn't believe how naïve I'd been.

'You know, Em. That's part of the reason why I moved here.' He looked up again and I watched with relief as his hand stopped moving. 'Your mum would have been happy staying in Belfast and getting married there, but I couldn't. It was too intolerant, and it made me too angry on Stephen's behalf.'

'Don't you miss Maimeó and Daideó?'

My dad started to pack away the board game, his tears having been blinked away and his air of confidence somewhat restored. 'Sometimes. But, honestly, I was so scared of revealing my sexuality to them that I avoided them as much as possible. That's not a relationship a child should have with their parents.'

Neither of us spoke as I helped him put away the rest of the Scrabble tiles. We then walked up the stairs together, pausing outside his and my mum's bedroom.

'Are you going to be okay?' I asked.

He nodded and squeezed my shoulder. 'Don't you worry about little old me.'

'Thanks for being honest.' I fidgeted as I waited for a reply.

'You too, mo stoirín.' He pulled me in for another hug. 'I'm sorry for stealing your spotlight.'

'Oh, don't be.' I held him tighter. 'It was an honour sharing it with you.'

Dad stepped back to look at me and we smiled at each other.

'Good luck with Alana.' He reached out to open his bedroom door and I started to walk down the hall to mine.

'Good luck with Mum.' With a twisting feeling in my gut, I knew that, while both of us needed the luck, my dad needed it more; his marriage was at risk. As much as I loved Alana, I knew I could always just pretend to be straight and keep her as my friend for the rest of my life. Now however, my dad didn't have that luxury.

Chapter 10

As hard as I tried, I couldn't get to sleep that night. The worst part was that I didn't know why; it could have been because I was worried about my parents, or because I was thinking about Alana getting her implants. It could also have been because I was worrying about the prospect of telling her how I felt. Whatever it was, it was infuriating. Until 5am, I alternated between lying down with my eyes squeezed shut, and reading about cochlear implants on my phone. Then, I just heaved myself out of bed and started to paint. The sun had already begun to rise, so I just opened my curtains instead of turning my light on.

After a few hours of adding colour to Alana's skin and freckles, I heard a door slam down the hall. I jumped at the sound, beyond relieved when I hadn't smudged any paint on the canvas. I then heard somebody stomp towards the bathroom and turn the shower on, before whoever was left in my parents' bedroom re-opened the door. They walked down the stairs and I held back my desire to follow them; no matter which parent it was, I knew I wouldn't be of any use to them. I didn't have the words to console my dad, and I couldn't even begin to empathise with my mum. Being caught in the middle really wasn't fun.

After I'd cleared my paints away and got dressed, the person in the bathroom finished up and returned to the bedroom, just as loudly as before. The hairdryer was turned on a few minutes later. I debated running downstairs to at least try and comfort my dad, but I settled for retrieving my phone from my pillow and sending him a heart emoji instead. After I had done so, I saw that I'd missed a video call from Alana during the night, and that she'd sent me a text at half past five.

Em, hey. Are you alright? Why are you up so early? xx

I wanted to kick myself for not checking my mobile.

Sorry Alana, I wasn't on my phone! Yeah, I'm fine thanks. Just family stuff. Are you okay? Xx

I nearly asked why she had been awake, then realised just how stupid a question that would have been. I blinked at my phone, my eyes widening as I took in the kisses that I'd added at the end of my text. And, more importantly, the kisses Alana had added at the end of hers. That had to mean something; we hadn't used kisses before.

I was so wrapped up in re-reading the two messages, that I didn't even hear my mum join my dad downstairs. It was only when I heard raised voices that I realised they'd reunited.

'You had years to tell me, Mark! Our whole marriage is built on a lie!'

I brought my hands up to my head and rubbed my temple.

'The fact that we love each other isn't a lie! Surely that's all that matters!'

'Maybe I'm not sure if I do love you.'

No. No, no, no. She didn't say that; she wouldn't say that. I wondered if there was any chance that I'd misheard my mum; her voice had been quieter when saying that last part after all. The next thing I knew, the front door had been opened and slammed shut again. I could just about hear my dad muttering in Gaelic before he left too. For the first time in my life, my parents left the house without saying goodbye to me. Even worse than that, they left without saying it to each other.

Though I tried not to, I began to think about how bitter my mum had sounded. I tried to figure out whether or not she really meant her words, and if she really was considering throwing away twenty years of marriage. As selfish as I felt, my thoughts then began to drift back to Alana and me. I knew that, if my mum was willing to leave my dad over his revelation, then it was fairly likely that Alana would leave me over mine; we'd known each other for a lot less time. Ironically though, I knew that seeing her was the one thing that would make me feel better, whether my love for her was a ticking time bomb or not.

I looked back at my phone to see that she'd replied.

I will be when I see you. Come over and we can go out?xx

I'll be there in two minutes. Xx

I tried to ignore how good it felt to add those kisses on the end, and brushed my teeth before heading to Alana's. She opened her door as I walked up the drive.

'You ready?' she asked.

'Always.' I already felt better. I didn't know where we were going, but I also knew that I didn't care as long as we were together.

'I brought breakfast,' Alana said, drawing my attention to a plastic bag she was carrying. 'I made a little picnic when I couldn't sleep last night.'

'Shall we go to the park then?' I noticed how her eyes seemed to droop as she watched my hands. She nodded nevertheless.

'Sure. Just don't throw up this time.'

We walked in silence, both of us looking at the pavement instead of each other. I guessed that Alana was thinking about her implants and I did the same, only allowing my worries about my parents to interfere every few minutes. The park was virtually empty when we reached it, save for a few people walking their dogs.

'How about here?' I signed, after we had walked a few metres from the gates. I gestured towards the grass underneath a cherry tree.

'Perfect.'

We sat beside each other, and I looked down at the flowers that had been ripped up and left on the ground.

Alana saw me looking at them and let out a sympathetic moan.

'I hate how kids do that,' she said. I looked up curiously. 'You know, they sit in parks and they rip up the grass. A lot of the time, they don't know any better. But it's still sad, don't you think? I mean look at all these daisies. They've been ripped up and left to die.'

'That's a horrible way of looking at it.' She was right, though.

'Yeah. But I guess nothing is too horrid to be made into something beautiful.' She clambered to her feet and began to pick up the abandoned daisies.

'Alana, can I tell you something?' I signed when she was sitting again, a pile of flowers in front of her. 'Something personal?' I hardly trusted myself to speak, but the early morning birdsongs and my lack of sleep made me painfully uninhibited.

'You can tell me anything.' She picked through the daises and pulled out one with a long stem. 'What's wrong?'

'Nothing's wrong,' I said slowly, aware that she wasn't watching my hands or reading my lips. 'But, well, after what you said yesterday, I came out to my parents.'

'You what?' The daisy slipped from Alana's fingers and she turned back to face me.

'I came out during game night.' My voice was so smooth that I almost thought it didn't belong to me. I squeezed my hands into fists, my nails slightly scratching my palms, to ensure I wasn't dreaming. 'I came out as bisexual.'

'You? Oh. I had no idea you were, I just, I didn't know.' I couldn't read Alana's expression at all, and I tried to figure out what I wanted her to say. I was beyond relieved that at least she wasn't accusing me of copying her. 'How did it go? Is that why you couldn't sleep?'

'It went okay.' Alana gave me a sad smile, as if she knew I wasn't telling the whole truth. 'Well, it went okay for me. But then my dad revealed that he's bisexual too, and my mum…' I tried to think of the signs I needed. 'Angry,' I signed eventually.

'Wait, your dad?' Alana frowned. 'So, you came out together? Did you know he was going to come out too?'

'I had no idea. Neither did my mum and she was not happy.'

'How did she react to you?'

'She didn't seem to understand completely, but she was fine. I'm more worried about how she argued with my dad this morning.'

Alana picked up a daisy and pushed her nail through its stem before threading another one through the hole. 'Parents argue. Don't worry about it.'

'Not mine.' I watched her work, grateful for the distraction. 'I can't help but feel like it's my fault, you know? If I hadn't have said anything –'

'If you hadn't have said anything, then you would still be living a lie. Your parents wouldn't know the real you and you wouldn't know your dad.' Alana looked up from her daisy chain making to smile at me, but for once she didn't manage to immediately reassure me. 'You did a really brave thing, Emily. I'm proud of you.'

'But what if they break up because of it?'

'You mean like my parents?' That was kind of exactly what I meant, but hearing Alana say it just made me feel guilty. I nodded. 'Emily, your family is nothing like mine, okay? Yes, my parents divorced after I came out. But, before that, my dad never appreciated my mum. He barely came home before midnight and he hardly acknowledged her when he was back anyway. He left because he wasn't a good person, not because I'm gay. I sometimes find it hard to believe, but it's true.

'And your dad is nothing like that; he smiles at your mum when she's not looking, and he doesn't change out of his work clothes when he gets home because he'd rather spend his time with her. He values her, and she would be stupid to throw that away. And if there's one thing I know about your mum, it's that she's not stupid.'

I felt myself inhale sharply, touched by the thought that Alana had paid attention to my family and that she was willing to comfort me.

'So, you think they're going to be okay?' I picked up one of Alana's flowers and curled it around my finger. When she didn't respond to me, I realised just how quietly I'd spoken and I repeated myself more clearly.

'I really do. They might fight, but so did Cathy and Heathcliff, and look at how that turned out.'

I tilted my head to the side as I thought back to *Wuthering Heights*. 'That turned out really badly.'

'Yeah, they probably weren't a good example.' Alana smiled, and, as I watched the way her eyes crinkled, I started to smile too. 'Are you glad that you came out to them, though? Obviously you're upset about the aftermath, but do you regret it?'

'I don't think I do; I think my dad needed to come out, and he wouldn't have done if I hadn't first.' Alana nodded as if she knew exactly what I meant, but I began to elaborate anyway. I spoke mainly, not knowing all of the signs I needed. 'He said nobody talked about being gay when he was young, and that that cost the life of someone he loved. When he said that, I knew I had made the right decision by being honest.'

'What do you mean?' Alana's face fell as she registered what I'd just said. I debated changing the subject, but in the back of my mind all I could think about was how Stephen deserved to be remembered. I knew that his death deserved to make a difference.

'We all need to talk about our sexualities more, don't you think? We need to let people know that love is beautiful in all its forms. Like, the whole idea of "you don't need to label yourself". I think that sometimes you do.' Alana nodded again, though I was pretty sure I'd stopped making sense. 'My dad loved a boy called Stephen Hope and he was gay. My dad is bisexual, as am I, and you're a lesbian. And that's okay.'

I made a mental note to stop making long speeches; though I could sign the latter half of what

I'd said, I realised I didn't make myself easy to understand.

'That's more than okay.' Alana added another daisy to her chain and somehow turned it into a crown, which she gently placed on top of my head. 'And I love bisexual Emily. The more love in this world, the better.'

It really felt as if her fingers lingered in my hair before she pulled them away, and I only broke our eye contact when I could feel myself starting to panic-sweat. I needed to get a grip on my feelings, but Alana had said the L word. Sure, love could mean a whole range of things, but when I used it about her I knew exactly what I meant. I was so busy over-thinking the statement *I love bisexual Emily,* that I didn't realise Alana had started to speak again.

'Emily?' She waved her hand in front of my face. 'You've drifted off.' That's because all I could think about was how much I loved her too. 'I was asking about James. Did you ever tell him you were bi?'

I wondered how long I'd been silent for.

'I didn't know I was when I was dating him,' I admitted. It wasn't until a comfortable silence settled, that I realised what I'd confessed to. I knew that it was only a matter of seconds before Alana realised that my sexual awakening had to have occurred after I met her. I tried to think of an explanation that would deter her from thinking that she was the cause of it. 'I think that hearing you talk about being gay helped me understand myself a little more.' Not bad; Alana seemed to buy it.

'Do you think that maybe that's why you didn't truly love him? Because you didn't really know yourself?' Or at least, if she had made the connection, she was hiding it well.

'Yeah, that could be it.' I tried not to focus on the fact that, if Alana liked me back, she would have admitted it by then. 'Though I also think that we just weren't right for each other. He was always nice to me, but he deserves someone different and I think I do too.' I wondered how miraculous someone would have to be to deserve Alana.

'You definitely do.' As she spoke, I found my eyes being drawn to her lips.

Maybe it was the summer heat and the fact that we were alone; maybe it was the topic of conversation or my lack of sleep, but something made me feel like I was back in my dream. It was almost as if I could feel the sand beneath me and hear the ocean. Neither of us said anything more; we just carried on looking at each other, and I forgot that Alana didn't like me back. I forgot how much I was potentially risking, and I closed my eyes before leaning forward and touching her lips with my own. When I felt the pressure of the action, it finally sunk in that I wasn't dreaming, and my eyes snapped open. I leant back and tried to gauge her reaction, not quite believing what I'd just done.

'I'm really sorry,' I said, quite remarkably seeing as the only thing going through my head was a constant stream of *shitwhatdidIdoshitwhatthehellshitshewillhatemenow.*

Alana blinked, her gaze not leaving mine. 'It's fine.'

'It's fine?' I wondered if I'd heard her correctly. I knew the fact that she was still sitting with me meant I hadn't completely ruined everything, but I hadn't expected what I'd just done to be called 'fine'; it simply wasn't. Her words lit a small flame of hope in me however, and I couldn't stop myself from smiling slightly as I signed. 'You mean…?'

'I mean it's fine. But we can't kiss, Emily.' And just like that, the flame was extinguished.

For the first time, I found myself unwilling to look at Alana; I couldn't bear the thought of seeing her beautiful skin creased into a frown because of something I'd done. As I scrambled to my feet, my smile fell, along with my daisy chain crown.

'Of course we can't. I'm really sorry, again.' I didn't even look back at her as I ran off, trying to hold back the sobs that I knew were coming. I thought I heard her call my name, but I resisted the urge to turn around; I was well aware that I'd made a huge, idiotic mistake and I didn't want to talk about it. I was still running when I reached my road, and my vision was so impaired by my tears that I ran straight into a person who was walking in the other direction. 'Sorry,' I mumbled. I tried to skirt past them.

'Emily?' I knew the voice before I could see who it belonged to.

'James?' Sure enough, it was him. His brows were furrowed as he looked at me, and just seeing him made me cry even more; it reminded me that Alana wasn't the first person to reject me that summer.

'Whoa, what happened?' He started to hold out his arms, as if he was offering me a hug but wanted to make sure he wasn't overstepping any boundaries. I immediately buried myself in his embrace, hoping that the comfort of another person would be enough to help me calm down.

'I just. I. I did such a stupid thing,' I managed to choke out. As soon as I realised my tears were going to stain his shirt, I pushed myself off him. 'I really messed things up and I don't know what to do and –'

For the second time that day, my lips found themselves pressed against someone else's. Although I was caught off guard, it didn't take long for me to start kissing back; it was as if nothing had changed and we were the same Emily and James who used to kiss each other on the field at lunchtime. It was familiar; it was safe. Our hands wrapped themselves around each other's bodies and they stayed like that until, after a few minutes, I pulled myself away again.

'Will you come back to mine, please?' I heard myself ask. I felt James' hot breath against my neck as he bent down to kiss it. 'We can carry on.' I fully expected him to say no; he was the one who'd ended things in the first place, and he'd probably only kissed me to calm me down. That's why I assumed I was imagining things again when he nodded.

'Sure.'

Chapter 11

I lay on my bed, my head in James' lap as I tried to look anywhere but out of the window. He curled my hair around his fingers, and the action would have been enough to lull me off to sleep if I hadn't been stressing about Alana.

'I'm sorry,' I said, after several minutes of neither of us talking. I considered the fact that, despite how long we had dated, this was the first time we'd even come close to sleeping together. 'I dragged you here and then didn't even make it worth your while.'

'Don't be sorry,' he replied instantly, prompting me to sit up and look him in the eyes. 'It was nice to see you, and you hardly dragged me here.'

I shuffled back so I was sitting beside him. There was a pause. 'So, how have you been?' I only just noticed that he'd had a haircut. I didn't like it.

'I'm great, thanks.' He smiled, ruffling his hair as if he had noticed me looking at it. 'I actually applied for late admission to a business college and got in.'

'That's amazing! Congratulations.' I tried my best to be pleased for him, biting back any snarky remarks about his gap year whim.

'And how are you?' His tone was soft. 'Don't try and tell me you're fine.'

I tried to figure out how I was, but nothing I'd ever felt was similar to my emotions in that moment; never before had I kissed a girl who happened to be my best friend and who probably didn't like me back. Never before had I had to deal with the repercussions of doing that. To top it off, never before had I thrown myself at my ex-boyfriend to distract myself from said girl.

'Were you crying about a boy?' His expression was neutral and his tone didn't hint towards any jealousy.

'Something like that.' Even though James had made me feel a tiny bit better, I still didn't want to admit what had just happened; I was too embarrassed and just wanted to wallow in pity on my own.

'Is there anything I can do?' His voice was quiet, and I looked over at my clock. It was nearly 5pm; we had been sitting in silence together for hours.

'Honestly, unless you want to face the wrath of my dad for breaking up with me, all I can suggest that you do is leave.' I gave him a wry smile as he stood up hurriedly, picking his jacket up off the floor.

'Right. Of course.' He slowly blew out his cheeks.

'Honestly James, I'm okay,' I lied, my eyes trailing over to the canvas of Alana. It was close to being finished, and seeing her face just made me want to start crying all over again. James must have noticed because I felt his hand on my shoulder a second later.

'Is she the reason you're crying?' All I could do was nod and hope he didn't start a sexuality inquisition. 'Ah. Honestly, I think you should go for it; you're amazing and just because we didn't work out, it doesn't mean you two won't.'

'Thanks.' I knew that I would have loved to hear those words a few days ago. I stood up and led him out of my room. 'Really, thank you. And good luck with everything.'

'You too.' We walked down the stairs together and James waited until he reached the front door before turning to me.

'Emily, you deserve the world, you know. Don't settle for anything less. I know I couldn't give it to you, but maybe she can.'

I watched him leave and, as I made my way back to my room, I thought about what he'd said. I thought about Alana. Then, I thought about the fact that I didn't want the world; I just wanted her.

I picked up my phone to see if she'd messaged me, resisting the nagging desire to text her first when I saw that she hadn't. Unsure of what else to do, I lay my ocean canvas down on the floor and decided to add the final touches to it; painting was always a good distraction. Plus, I figured that I might as well finish what I'd started, even if I never saw Alana again to give it to her.

As I was adding flecks of white to the tips of the waves, I heard the front door open and a low hum of voices; my parents must have come home at the same time. I braced myself for their mutterings to turn to shouts, but they never did. I finished painting, the canvas finally complete, and tried to hear what was happening.

'No, Mark. I really am sorry,' my mum said over the rustle of plastic bags. She'd probably spent all day comfort shopping. 'I shouldn't have reacted the way I did.' I knew that her confession was promising, but I didn't let myself get my hopes up; I knew that she would have more to say. 'But I'm sure that you can imagine how surprised I was.'

My dad's voice was quieter than hers. 'I know, and I'm sorry for telling you like I did. I've just been so stressed with work, and I felt like letting go of that secret might help a little. Besides, I didn't want Emily to feel completely alone.'

'You don't think she does, do you?' I tensed at my mum's high-pitched tone. Part of me was grateful that she cared enough to worry about me, but a different part of me wanted her to focus on my dad. 'Should we be doing something about her?'

If my dad replied, his voice was quieter than the noise of whatever was being put away. I heaved myself up off the floor and went to join them.

'Hey.' Their heads both snapped up to look at me. 'Were you talking about me?'

'No,' said my mum, just as my dad said the opposite. I reached into one of the carrier bags and started to unload its contents into the fridge.

'I heard a bit of what you were saying,' I confessed, squeezing a milk carton into the door. We already had two in there. 'And I want you to know that I'm okay.' I went to store the eggs too, but saw that we already had a full carton. 'I don't need you to do anything for me.' We also already had two tubs of butter. 'But, why did you go shopping? We don't need any of this.'

'I popped into Vellichor to see Mr Costas, and Linda asked me to pick some things up for her.' My mum began to fill the kettle. 'That was her bag.'

'Oh.' I looked down at the Lurpak I was holding. 'Right. Okay.' I took the milk and eggs back out of the fridge.

'Speaking of Linda, aren't you meant to be with Alana today?' my mum asked. I saw my dad freeze out of the corner of my eye. 'I thought you were having a sleepover tonight.'

'Yeah, what happened?' My dad turned to face me.

I tapped my foot on the floor, willing myself to make up for six years of missed teenage rebellion. To, for the first time, lie to my parents about what I'd done.

'We went to the park and I had to come home because…' I could see my dad's eyes close slightly, and it was like I could feel the pity radiating from him. 'Because I got my Dolmio day.' I cringed at my use of my mother's old euphemism, then at the fact that I hadn't been able to go a full summer without using the period excuse. At least something about me was still predictable, I noted.

'You did?' My mum's voice was gentle, and she walked over to pat me on the shoulder. 'Honey, this is why you need to track your cycle. We have a perfectly good calendar over there.' My eyes fluttered over to the wall. My mum wrote the letters 'P.S' in bright red ballpoint every twenty-eight days, and my dad and I always joked that we paid more attention to it than her so we could track her moods. There was no way I was about to add my own cycle.

'You did?' My dad's expression was neutral again, aside from his raised eyebrows. It was as if he knew better than to take my words at face value. I wondered what it would be like to have a father who was grossed out by natural biology.

'Yep.' I nodded furiously, unpacking another bag of shopping so that I could focus my eyes somewhere else other than on him. 'And I didn't want to stay overnight whilst I'm on in case. You know. Leakage.'

'Right. Though your dad and I had planned to go out for tea so we can talk things over. You're more than welcome to join us.' My mum's words made my heart feel it was swelling; I was so happy that they were willing to communicate with each other, that I almost forgot about my own issues with Alana. Specifically, the fact that she'd made it clear we could never have a relationship like my parents

'No, you two have fun. I'm going to sit in front of a nice horror film and eat meringues.'

'Don't you usually binge watch rom-coms during shark week?' My dad looked at me pointedly.

'I'm not really in the mood for them today.' At least there was truth in that sentence. 'You know what? I think I'm just going to go to bed early and try to sleep my cramps off.'

I hobbled upstairs, bent at the stomach, and ignored my mum as she asked me to take Mrs Wilson's bag next door.

Before getting into bed, I knelt down beside my ocean painting again. I stared at the waves, wondering if Alana would ever even see the finished piece. In a matter of seconds, tears were dripping from my eyes straight onto the canvas.

'Shit.' I dabbed at the droplets that had fallen on dry areas, and watched as the others dissolved on the canvas. I was too pre-occupied to even acknowledge the fact I'd sworn. 'Well, painting with tears is a first.'

I climbed on top of my bed and turned onto my side. Within seconds, I caught sight of the photo booth pictures from weeks ago on my bedside cabinet. I leaned over to pick up the strip and looked at it, a shaky sigh escaping from my lips. Even if Alana and I somehow managed to stay friends, I knew that she would never want to get that close to me again. I crushed the photo strip up in my hand and threw it across the room.

Chapter 12

I woke up at 7am the next day, still on top of my duvet and wearing my clothes from the day before. I couldn't remember what I'd been dreaming about, but my hair was plastered to my face with sweat, and I'd somehow managed to kick my shoes onto the floor. Without looking through the window, I grabbed my towel and shuffled to the bathroom for a shower.

It was nearly two hours later by the time I'd got dried and dressed, which meant I could still make it in time for Alana's operation. That was, if she even wanted me there. I tried to figure out if that was even remotely likely, but found myself walking down the street to the bus stop regardless. I didn't even notice whether the Wilsons car was still on their drive; I was too wrapped up in thinking about what was going to happen to Alana. I wanted her to be able to hear again, far more than I wanted her to be in love with me, and I knew that whatever was going to happen would do so even if I wasn't there to witness it. The bus arrived just as I debated turning back, and I hopped on with a grimace.

At ten minutes to 10, I walked into the hospital. I scanned the waiting room, momentarily alarmed when I didn't see a mass of curly red hair. I looked once more, desperately hoping I wasn't too late, and very nearly missed Alana again; she was sitting in the corner of the room, her hair pulled back in a messy ponytail. Her bright hearing aids looked almost garish against her even paler than usual complexion. She wasn't looking at me; she didn't seem to be looking at anything in particular, so I just stood awkwardly for a minute, shifting my bodyweight from one leg to the other.

'Emmy, is that you?' Mrs Wilson walked towards me, a nurse following a few steps behind her. 'You came!' She flung her arms around me, her un-brushed hair tickling my cheek.

'I did.'

I watched as the nurse made her way over to Alana and tapped her arm. She signed that it was time, just as Mrs Wilson pulled away from me.

We followed Alana and the nurse through several long corridors, neither of them acknowledging my presence, and eventually we stopped outside an office. There was a silver sign on the door reading 'Doctor Rivers', and the nurse gave an encouraging smile to Alana before knocking. She left again. Alana gave me a small nod as a voice from inside the room told us to come in.

Doctor Rivers was older than I'd imagined, with thinning, wavy grey hair down his back. He gestured at the three chairs in front of his desk, but didn't move from his own seat. Alana sat in the middle, directly across from him, as Mrs Wilson and I sat either side of her. The seats were made of a dark blue plastic that felt far too reminiscent of school chairs, and it was impossible to sit comfortably on them.

'Good afternoon,' the doctor said. I looked over to Mrs Wilson, who shared the same worried expression as me. I wondered if she too was unnerved by him not knowing the time. 'Thanks for coming in.' He spoke with a harsh Scottish accent and clasped his fingers together as he did so. My gaze fell to his desk and the leaflets that were covering it. Each was a different colour in a too-bright shade, and they all displayed the same gaudy font. Every title related to hearing loss and how to cope with it. 'How are you feeling today, Alana?'

'I'm feeling fine, thank you.' Her cracking voice suggested otherwise. Mrs Wilson smiled at her. 'I'm ready for the implants.'

'That's good.' He smiled too, but it looked more like a twitch than a conscious response. 'Though Alana, you know we couldn't guarantee that you could have them.'

I looked over to Alana and could feel myself beginning to frown. I watched her shoulders rise as she inhaled.

'I know that, but –'

'You can follow conversations with just your hearing aids; you don't need this permanent surgery.' Doctor Rivers emphasised the word permanent, and a fleck of spit left his mouth as he did so. I could see Alana's hands grip the sides of her chair.

'I have to lip read too.' Her gaze was stony, and I didn't envy the doctor being on the receiving end of it. 'My old doctor said I could have the implants if my nerves weren't too damaged. You said they aren't.'

I heard a small tapping noise, and turned to see that Mrs Wilson's fingernail was bouncing on the edge of her chair. Alana didn't react to it.

'Then I said you needed another consultation with me.' Doctor Rivers had a sip of water from the glass on his desk. 'I'm sorry, Alana. Whilst you benefit from the hearing aids, you don't qualify for free cochlear implants.'

My heart began to feel heavy in my chest as I took in his words. I tried to take a deep breath, but my lungs felt restricted, as if somebody was squeezing as much air out of them as they could.

'We can't even begin to afford paying for them,' Alana whispered. She relaxed her hands and slumped back in her chair. I watched as her eyes closed and her lips pressed together. I watched, and I waited for her to come alive again, to fight like I knew she could.

'I can refer you to support groups in the area,' said Doctor Rivers. I tore my eyes away from Alana in order to glare at him. My lungs started to loosen, and I resisted the urge to scream. 'Nurse Eva can come back and show you how to sign up.'

Without waiting for Alana to respond, Doctor Rivers rang for the nurse to lead her away. Just like that, a summer of waiting was wasted. Mrs Wilson and I stayed seated as we watched them leave.

'Doctor, are you sure there's nothing you can do?' she asked when the door had closed again. 'You did lead us to believe the operation was going ahead.'

'Nothing, I'm afraid.' He collected his leaflets into a pile and handed them to her. 'Is that all?'

'I suppose so.' She took the leaflets without thanking him, then held the door open for me. Neither of us said goodbye. It was strange seeing Linda be so quiet and apathetic too, and I started to wish for the larger than life Wilsons to come back. More than that, I wished for the Doctor to realise he'd made a mistake and that Alana's operation could go ahead after all. I waited for him to check his obnoxiously large pile of paperwork and come running after us. He didn't.

'Thanks for coming today,' Linda said, after we'd returned to the waiting room and sat down. Her hand grabbed mine and she squeezed it. 'It really means a lot to me and Al.'

'I wouldn't dream of not being here.' I could see a pool of water in the corner of her eye and my breath hitched. 'And she'll be okay.'

I began to repeat that line over and over in my head as we waited; it was as if I'd only just realised how serious the situation was. I'd been so wrapped up in my own feelings that I'd forgotten about what Alana was going through. For weeks, I'd been concerned about our future together, either as friends or more, and I'd never once thought about what the immediate aftermath of that day would be. Without even meaning to, I brought my other hand up to my mouth and ripped off a hangnail I could feel by my thumb.

After a few minutes that easily could have been hours, I looked up at the clock. It was twenty past 10;

the doctor hadn't even tried to stretch out the consultation. I looked down again, then back up.

'A watched clock,' said Mrs Wilson after I'd looked down and up twice more, 'will tell you to fuck off.' I raised my eyebrows and turned to her, but she wasn't smiling. 'She'll be back soon, love.'

I hated the thought of Alana being alone with a nurse she didn't know, especially in that moment. When I couldn't bear staring at the wall in front of me anymore, I took out my phone and tried to look up some more BSL signs, but there was no signal. I settled for watching my leg bounce up and down.

Mrs Wilson squeezed my hand again after a few seconds, and I tried to be still. As I looked up at her, she seemed to cheer up a little, however her expression quickly fell again as she saw something behind me. I shifted in my seat to see what she was looking at.

Alana was shuffling towards us. She'd taken her hair out of her ponytail and it covered the sides of her face. She had a stack of leaflets, similar in size to Mrs Wilson's.

'Lana…' I began, though I had no idea what to say. She wasn't actually looking at me, and I could hear Mrs Wilson trying to steady her breathing behind me. I willed myself to be the strong one.

'Mrs Wilson?' The nurse hurried over from the direction Alana had come from. Her eyes were wide and she looked a lot more sympathetic than the doctor had done. 'Alana is a bit upset so, if you like, I can give you the information about support groups for her.'

Mrs Wilson looked to Alana, who nodded slightly. She walked away with the nurse and, though I knew my mind was devoid of any practical ideas, I tried to think of something I could do to make Alana feel better. When she still hadn't moved after a few more seconds of silence, I grabbed her hand and started to walk towards the lift.

'Where are we going?' she asked wearily, as if she didn't really care. I didn't answer, instead choosing to press the button that called the elevator down. I hoped my idea would work, knowing I'd be completely stuck for a plan if it didn't. 'Emily, I'm tired and I want to go home.'

I bit my lip, but ignored her as the lift doors opened. I pulled Alana inside and pressed the button for the roof, acknowledging how it felt like years since the last time we'd been in an elevator together. Once again, I was too distracted to worry about some freak failure happening and leaving us trapped.

'I just want to show you something,' I said eventually. I saw that Alana had tearstains on her cheeks and I swallowed back any more words. I found myself thinking back to the first time I saw her in her window.

When the lift stopped, we walked out and onto the hospital roof. There was a high stone wall lining the edge that I had to tiptoe to look over, and Alana followed me towards it. The air was a lot colder than it had been in the morning, with a few dark clouds now in the sky. Alana craned her neck to look down at the street.

Although there were hundreds of people, all talking to each other, and there were buses and cars, all I could hear was a low hum. I saw a couple standing outside a shop, both raising their arms and stamping their feet. As hard as I tried, I couldn't make out their voices at all.

'Emily, how is this going to make me feel better?' Alana's voice was hoarse as she looked at me.

I signed from my place in front of her. 'We're so high up, I can't hear anything either.' She looked away for a brief second. 'Alana,' I continued, despite my better judgement. 'I have no idea what you're going through, but I never want you to feel alone. And I know you're still losing your hearing, but I want you to know that you're never going to lose me.' *Unless, of course, you hate me because I kissed you.*

'Thank you.'

Mrs Wilson drove us back in absolute silence; she didn't even turn the radio on. I tried to imagine living the rest of my life like that and I had to fight to keep back the tears; I was not going to let myself cry again. It was Alana's tragedy, not mine, and I didn't have any right to be upset. I tried to hug her goodbye after we got out of the car, but she just walked straight past me towards her house. Mrs Wilson patted my shoulder.

'She'll be back to her usual self soon,' she told me as she locked her car. 'Thanks again for coming.'

'It was no problem.'

Linda followed Alana inside and I let myself into my own house, where my parents were starting to lay out food on the table. My mum wasn't wearing an apron, though there was one lying on the tiles. It was blue, and read *'The Best is Yet to Crumb'* below a loaf of bread.

'Perfect timing, honey!' she said, her cheeks flushed and hair tousled. I looked at my dad, whose shirt was untucked and whose face had remnants of red lipstick on it. The same lipstick that was smudged around my mother's lips. *Ew*. As gross as it was, I thought, at least they had made up and something good had come out of the day.

'What's for tea?' I asked, looking anywhere but at them. Of course, I wanted them to be in love again, but I didn't really want to see the evidence of it.

'It's... it's...' Mum looked at my dad, squealing slightly as she took in his appearance. She lifted the bottom corner of her shirt and used it to dab at his face. 'Chicken. Chicken and salad.'

'I'll get some plates then.'

In a matter of minutes, we were all eating quietly. Well, my parents were; I couldn't bring myself to swallow anything and just kept chewing the same piece of chicken over and over until it basically disintegrated on my tongue.

'Did Alana get her implants?' my dad asked softly.

I closed my eyes. 'No.'

'Oh the poor girl. She must feel so disappointed.'

'It's a shame,' my mum added, winning the award for the understatement of the century. 'She's such a nice girl too.' I pushed my food around my plate as my dad hummed in agreement. 'Do you think I should make another basket for them?'

'Mum. Alana doesn't want cakes, trust me.' I glared down at my food as if the lettuce and breadcrumbs were to blame for Alana's misfortune.

'Emily, we know that. We just want to help in some way.' I could sense that my dad was looking at me as he spoke, but I refused to move my gaze.

'Yeah, well, so do I.'

'Emily, what happened between you two yesterday?' That was my mum, asking the question I had been dreading. 'You're not really on your period, are you?'

Her words were enough to break my focus, and I felt the tears I'd been holding back since Dr Rivers' office finally come out. I dropped my cutlery on the table, not even flinching when they clattered loudly.

'I've done something horrible,' I said between hiccups, a salty taste on my lips. I'd done an awful lot of crying in those twenty-four hours. 'And I think Alana hates me now and it's all my fault.'

My dad pushed his chair back and walked around the table to kneel on the floor beside me. 'Emily, what on earth do you mean?'

'You know I said I thought she liked me back?' I looked up to see both of my parents nodding. Their concerned faces made me feel even worse; there I was, stealing the sympathy from Alana. 'Well, I was wrong. I kissed her and she didn't want me to. It was selfish and stupid, and it was the day before she was meant to have her implants and I made it all about me.'

My dad clasped his hands around mine as my mum got up from the table and walked over to the kitchen counter.

'So, of course, I was mortified and I ended up running back here. I left her alone before one of the biggest days of her life because of a stupid unrequited crush.'

'Emily, you can't help the fact that you were upset,' my dad said. I crossed my arms over my chest, thankful that my tears were finally falling less gradually. I didn't care that I was upset; I cared that I was a terrible friend. 'Besides, did she tell you that she doesn't like you like that?'

My lips parted slightly. It wasn't like my dad to not listen to me. 'Dad, she didn't have to. She pushed me off and said that we couldn't kiss.' I used the sleeve from my jacket to try and dry my face.

'Yes, but –'

'And then I walked into James,' I continued. I knew that mentioning him would distract my dad enough to stop him giving me false hope about Alana.

My mum, who had been rooting in one of the cupboards below the sink, straightened up and joined us again at the table. She presented a box of tissues to me. 'You walked into whom?'

I removed one of the tissues and started to wipe my eyes properly. 'It's fine. He was fine. He actually helped me think straight.' My mum cocked her head to the side. 'Think straight, Mum. Not be straight.'

'In that case, I don't think you should give up on Alana.' My dad stood again and patted my hair. 'You should hear what she has to say.'

'But what if she hasn't got anything to say to me?' I was more than willing to continue being friends with Alana, even if that meant dying inside every time it reoccurred to me that I'd never date her. The more I thought about it, however, the more I felt like she probably never wanted to see me again.

'You know what I've always told you Emily.' He returned to his chair. 'You can either give in, or you can give it all that you've got.'

'But –'

'Don't argue with your father, Emily,' my mum said. 'He's right. You should go and you should get the girl before you regret missing your chance.'

'And if she doesn't like me back?'

'At least you'll know. And besides, you should never feel threatened by ifs.'

After I'd forced down more food, I neatened myself up in the bathroom and told myself that, if I didn't go and see Alana right that second, I might never be brave enough to. I announced to my parents that I was giving it all I had, and I marched next door, trying to keep my head up high. The clouds I'd seen from the hospital roof had doubled, and the tell-tale raindrops from the start of a storm were beginning to fall. I hoped that it wasn't pathetic fallacy, as much as Emily Bronte would have liked it to be.

Chapter 13

I knocked on the door, freezing cold rain dripping down my neck, and I rehearsed all of the things I could say. I was going to start with an apology; move into an explanation; wait for Alana's reaction. By the time the door opened however, I had lost my ability to think coherently.

'Emily, I'm really sorry but Alana wants to be left alone tonight.' I hadn't even noticed that Mrs Wilson was wearing make-up in the hospital, but she had clearly taken it off by then; the bags under her eyes were worryingly dark and her lips looked almost grey.

'Please. I won't stay long, I just need to see her.'

She must have been as tired as she looked, for she simply opened the door wider and let me in. I took my time walking up the stairs, trying to remember my plan.

When I entered Alana's room, I saw her sitting on top of her pillow. Her knees were under her chin with her arms wrapped around them, and her eyes were closed. I made my way over slowly, before sitting beside her. She opened her eyes but didn't say anything. Her hair was loose now, and already curling again, and her entire face was tinged red. Despite how small and sad she looked, she was still unmistakeably Alana. For some reason, that surprised me.

I tried to control my shaky breathing enough to talk. 'I'm sorry you couldn't have the implants,' I said, signing at the same time.

'You shouldn't be; it wasn't your fault.'

'Then I'm sorry that I kissed you,' I blurted out, unable to help myself. I glared at my hands as if they had translated my words of their own accord.

'Don't be sorry for that either.' I frowned as Alana sighed and brushed her hair behind her ears. She hadn't put her hearing aids back in. 'I understand why you did it,' she began, signing too. 'We were talking about you coming out, which I know must be really confusing for you, and then we moved on to James and you were missing him. I was there; you don't have to explain.'

I stuttered in my eagerness to get my words out and tried to keep my gestures clear. 'No, no, that's not it. Alana, I –'

'I saw you kiss him after the picnic,' she interrupted, looking up at me. 'I came over to your house to apologise and I saw you both.'

Of course she did; that was just my luck.

'Nothing else happened,' I tried to sign, but Alana just looked down.

'Emily, it doesn't matter if something did. You dated him for months; you're bound to still have feelings for him.'

I really wished that Alana could hear then, just so I could confidently explain what had happened. 'Nothing else happened because I realised I was making a mistake.' As always, I fingerspelt the words

I didn't know. 'We got to my room and James could tell that something was wrong. I don't have any feelings for him at all.'

'So, why did you kiss me?'

I felt my heart beginning to beat faster. It was my moment.

'I guess, I thought that you wanted me to. But I don't want it to ruin our friendship, so we can forget about it.'

Alana uncurled herself slightly. 'Did *you* want the kiss?'

I made my hand into a fist and moved it as if I was knocking on a door. 'Yes.' She didn't respond. 'But I'm sorry; I shouldn't have done it. I know we're just friends and I'm sorry.'

'Please stop saying sorry.' Her voice sounded so tired that I stopped trying to explain myself. I listened to the rain dancing on the window before she spoke again. 'Emily, you learnt a whole new language just to talk to me. You accept me without question and you're probably the nicest person I've ever met; you never need to apologise for anything.'

Hearing those words should have delighted me, but I felt a strange pang in my chest; I knew that Alana was just expressing gratitude for our friendship and something in me still wanted more.

'But you don't like me like that, and I should have checked.' I wanted to continue, but Alana placed her hands on mine and stopped me.

'I never said I don't like you like that.'

As I looked at her, I felt myself growing hot and my fingers fidgeted beneath hers.

'You said that we couldn't kiss,' I signed eventually, after freeing my hands.

'Because I wanted to wait.' Alana was now sitting cross-legged and frowning slightly. As she leaned towards me, she told me that she'd had feelings for me since we met. She said she'd never known love like it, to blossom so quickly between two strangers. Every so often, she moved back slightly, as if she was trying to gage my reaction. I knew I had a ridiculous grin on my face; I had never felt as relieved as I did then. 'So, when you kissed me,' she continued. 'I was just surprised. I wanted to get my implants before focusing on us.'

And then the guilt kicked in again; I could have picked any day to act on my feelings and I'd chosen the one before she had a life-changing opportunity.

'How do you feel now?' I signed, hoping more than anything that my impulsiveness hadn't affected her feelings. Alana was admitting that she liked me back and I knew I wouldn't be able to cope if I had caused that to change.

'Now, I've had the worst night and worst day of my life. I thought you came to the hospital because you felt obliged to and that I'd never see you again because you were back with James.' She looked down and began to twiddle her thumbs. 'If I absolutely have to, I can deal with losing my hearing for good. But I can't deal with losing you if there's any other choice.'

'I'm really confused,' I admitted, not letting myself get my hopes up. For nearly an entire summer, I had been wishing that Alana felt the same way about me as I did about her. Now that she was saying she did, though, I simply couldn't believe her.

My words made her smile and the spark finally returned to her eyes. 'Emily, I love you too. Do you want me to spell it out?' She proceeded to do so with her fingers, and I started to laugh. I had no idea what to say, something that Alana caught on to fairly quickly. 'You were really cool when you found out about Eve the other day,' she told me. 'And I nearly told you how I felt then, but I didn't want to risk creeping you out. The second I saw you in your window all those weeks ago, I knew that you would be the one to make me fall in love again.'

'Really?'

'Yeah. Except, I was pretty sure that you were straight.'

'So was I,' I signed. I laughed again; after just a few short minutes, I felt like all my worries had disappeared. 'I can't believe that you like me back.'

Then, before I could take in what was happening, Alana leaned forward, her face inches from mine. She paused for a second, as if waiting for permission, and I gently pressed my lips to hers.

Films always describe great kisses as being like fireworks, but that doesn't even come close to what kissing Alana was like. It had the sparks and it had the wonder of a firework display, but it also had so much more. When I pulled away to look into her eyes, I could still feel it. The amazement was still there and when she brought her lips back up to mine, it was like nothing I'd ever felt before. Kissing James had been fun, but it was nothing compared to kissing Alana.

'Wow,' she whispered when our lips separated. She pulled away, her eyes shut. 'I –'. They flickered back open.

'You?' I pulled my tongue out at her, tipsy with happiness and amazed that she was the speechless one. 'Was there something you wanted to say?'

She shook her head slightly, her expression dazed. After a pause, she looked at me with twinkling eyes.

'I love you,' she said simply. She nodded after she did so. 'Yes, that's what I wanted to say. I love you.'

'I love you too.'

'So that dream you had about me months ago?' Alana was clearly trying not to smirk. 'Was that..?'

I hesitated; by telling her the truth and admitting I'd imagined us kissing for months, I could be risking whatever we had just started. Despite that, I couldn't bring myself to lie to her.

'That was how I knew I liked you,' I signed. 'In it, we didn't just talk. We kissed.' I watched Alana's reaction through narrowed eyes, relaxing when she simply beamed at me.

'So, it was a dream, all a dream, and you wish me to know that I inspired it?'

'Oh, we're back to Dickens now, are we?'

'Well I'm sure that's where it all began.'

Alana kissed me again, and I kissed her back without fear of rejection and I knew I had never felt happier than I did in that moment; I was there, and she was too, and that was more than enough. As I closed my eyes, I heard the rain outside get even heavier as it fell on her bedroom window. It was the perfect background music, and I kissed Alana all that much more as if to make up for her not being able to hear it. I wished that I could give her hearing back to her, but all I could give was myself and I vowed to always try and be enough.

'So how do you feel?' she asked me, when we eventually pulled apart again. She lay back on her bed and I paused before joining her, then signed my answer in the space above our heads.

'As far from Miss Havisham as I could possibly be.'

'Nobody in their right mind would leave you at the altar.'

Chapter 14

After running down Alana's drive and back up mine, I had been completely drenched by rain. Despite that, I couldn't have felt warmer. My parents took one look at my huge grin and pulled me in for a hug. My mum only cringed slightly at my soaking wet clothes.

'Well done, mo stoirín,' my dad said, resting his chin on the top of my head. 'Just remember to love yourself as much as you love her.'

'I will do.'

After I had got into bed, my phone beeped with a text message.

Shall we re-do our breakfast picnic in the morning? I'll try not to scare you off this time xx

That sounds perfect! I'll bring the food xx

I dreamt about Alana again that night, but we weren't on a beach. Instead, we were in a library, sitting at a table in complete silence. I was opposite her, a copy of *To Kill a Mockingbird* in my hand, and my feet were intertwined with hers. Every so often, I glanced up just to look at her. After a few minutes, Alana looked up at the same time and she set her book down to sign at me.

'I love you,' she mouthed.

'I love you too,' I said, speaking without thinking. The loud 'shushing' of a librarian woke me up.

It was 8am and, in our morning texts, we'd agreed to go to the park at 10, so I had a shower and looked in my wardrobe to find a suitable outfit. After looking for what could have been hours based on how boring it was, I found a green high-waisted skater skirt and a black crop top. I'd never worn the shirt before, mainly because I'd always been self-conscious about my stomach, but I felt brave that morning. More than that, I felt indestructible.

My mum was already in the kitchen when I went downstairs, her apron a pastel yellow colour and covered with pictures of ovens, microwaves and hobs. It read '*Let the Heaters Heat*'.

'Hey, Mum.' I took a plastic tub out of one of the drawers. Judging from what I could smell, she was cooking bacon. 'I'm having breakfast in the park with Alana today.'

'That's great!' She pointed towards a roll of tinfoil on the counter. 'I cooked far too much food, so you can make some sandwiches and wrap them in that to take with you.'

I smiled my thanks as I filled the tub with grapes and strawberries, jumping when I heard a voice behind me.

'There's no such thing as too much food.' It was my dad, once again wearing his pyjamas. I'd never seen him take so many days off in one summer. He began to butter slices of bread beside my mum, humming some show tune as he did so.

'There is when it means Emily can then take some for her and Alana.' My mum opened the oven door and used a tea towel to remove the tray. Both my dad and I sniffed the air before grinning at each other.

Five minutes later, when I was armed with a plastic bag and four bacon sandwiches, I walked up to Alana's driveway. She was sitting on her wall and waiting for me, a blanket in her hand.

'Good morning,' she signed. She said it too, but the wind had begun to pick up and I couldn't quite catch her words.

'Good morning.' Alana squinted as her hair blew into her eyes. I reached forward to brush it out of her face before we began walking.

'To the park?'

'To the park.'

We decided to sit under the cherry tree again, Alana insisting that she wanted the spot to hold happier memories than those of her pushing me away. She spread out the blanket so we could sit down without getting damp from the grass, and the wind finally began to subside. We ate as the sun started to become visible.

'I love bacon,' Alana murmured, her mouth full of bread. It was completely unfair that she still looked gorgeous.

'I do too,' I signed, after finishing the sandwich I was eating. Alana giggled and brought her palm down to the ground. She waved it over the top of the grass, sending dew and rain in every direction.

'Thank you for the food,' she said after a while. I smiled, searching for something to say in reply. 'This is weird, isn't it?' she continued.

'What?' I'd been hoping that she hadn't noticed the awkwardness of the silence.

'All of a sudden, we can't speak to each other. It's weird.'

'I can speak to you,' I signed desperately, terrified that whatever we had was going to be deemed too much trouble than it was worth.

Alana closed her eyes. 'I think we need to talk about the elephant in the room.'

'But we're not in a room.'

She let out a groan, but I could see her lips turning upwards. 'I said that I love you, and you said that you love me.'

'Yeah.'

'Well, that didn't make things awkward; what has made things awkward is the fact that we haven't progressed from that. We can't still be friends.'

'We can't?' I tried to figure out how something so new could already be breaking apart.

'Friends who love each other? That doesn't seem like it will work out well.' Alana opened the box of fruit and took out a grape, throwing it from one hand to another. 'I think, and you can say no, I think that it might be better if we became something else. Something like girlfriends?'

As she looked up, her eyes darting from mine to her hand, it took all of my strength to stop myself from laughing in relief.

'I would very much like to be your girlfriend,' I told her, spelling out the last word as I didn't know how to sign it. Alana popped the grape into her mouth and brushed her finger against her cheek. It was the sign for 'girl', except she did it twice, and quicker than I'd ever seen 'girl' be signed before.

'Girlfriend,' she said eventually.

'Girlfriend.' I repeated the action.

Alana then lay back on the blanket, her hair displayed around her face almost like a mane. 'I'd very much like that too,' she said softly, looking at the sky. 'You know, this world is wonderful. And you just made it even better.'

I got in the same position as her, not even worrying about how I might look to anybody walking past, and Alana started to list the things she thought made the world wonderful. She started with the sky; then the birds; the grass; the wind. Content with the sound of her voice and the knowledge that we were together, I closed my eyes.

We lay there for a while: her in love with life, and me in love with her. I even fell asleep at one point, and was startled awake by a dog barking. As I sat up, I saw that the park had begun to fill with parents and their kids, destroying the tranquillity I'd been enjoying. I also saw that Alana was no longer beside me.

'Alana?' I shouted, just as a gust of wind blew my words away. 'Alana?' I jumped onto my feet and turned in a circle, my head filling with hundreds of scenarios that could have happened. The barking became deafening, and my vision began to blur as I moved.

Suddenly, she was back in front of me. 'Emily, what's wrong?'

'Oh my God.' I threw my arms around her, ridiculously relieved that she was fine. 'Please don't do that,' I signed, after pulling away.

'I was putting our rubbish in the bin.' She gestured towards the area the plastic bag had been occupying. She still had the fruit tub, but she put it down by her feet to start signing. 'And I didn't want to wake you. I didn't expect you to miss me so much.'

'Well, I did,' I signed, exhaling slowly. My heartrate was finally returning to its normal speed. 'I was terrified.'

As Alana laughed, I leant forward to kiss her, still amazed that that was something I could do, but I stopped when I heard someone approach us. We turned to see a man of around thirty holding a young boy's hand. I braced myself for a lecture on PDAs, willing myself not to die of embarrassment.

'Hi, I'm sorry to interrupt. My name's Michael and this is my stepson Daniel.' Michael spoke softly, so I had to concentrate to hear him over the noise of the park. As he walked closer to us, he stumbled over his own feet and I noticed that his face was flushing. I hoped against hope that we weren't about to experience a homophobic rant; I knew I would probably start crying. Swallowing the lump in my throat, I translated Michael's words for Alana as Daniel looked up at me with wide eyes. After I had finished, the man continued to speak.

'Daniel is Deaf. I'm still learning sign language myself, so I wasn't sure what exactly he was saying, but I think he wanted to say hello to you two.'

I looked back at the little boy with the captivated gaze, who was now concentrating on Alana. Again, I signed Michael's words. After I'd done so, Alana knelt down in front of Daniel.

'Hi, Daniel. I'm Alana and I'm deaf too,' she signed, her lips only mouthing the words rather than saying them. The little boy pointed at me before replying in BSL.

'I saw you signing with your friend.'

'She's called Emily. She's very nice. She learnt sign language to talk to me.'

'My new dad is very nice too. He is learning sign language for me.' I stole a glance at Michael to see if he was able to follow the conversation and, judging by the grin on his face, he was.

'I'm sorry for disturbing you both,' he whispered, still watching his stepson as he giggled at a joke Alana was telling him.

'You don't need to be sorry,' I said, equally fixated on the two. Alana was laughing too, her gestures big and confident. 'It was more than worth it.'

Alana and I stayed in the park for a few more hours after that, alternating between sitting on the swings and avoiding the sun; Alana didn't want to burn. The whole time, though, my mind kept wandering back to Michael and Daniel. Even as we began the walk back towards our houses, I found myself smiling as I thought about them.

'Okay, what is up with you?' Alana asked eventually. 'You have had this adorable little grin on your face for ages. Why?'

I tried not to be too distracted by the fact that Alana just called me adorable.

'You said you wanted to be a teacher, didn't you?'

Any trace of affection was suddenly gone from her face. 'Emily, can we not talk about this please?'

'But Alana, I saw you with Daniel; You would be an amazing teacher!' We stood still next to a bus stop so I could sign for her, though Alana's face was getting as red as her hair. I carried on regardless. 'Didn't you see how happy he was that he could talk to you? You could make other kids that happy too!'

'Please don't push this,' she said, barely making eye contact with me. 'I told you I don't want to teach Deaf kids. I have to live with –' She gestured towards her ears. 'This. I don't have a choice. But I do have a choice about who I spend my time with, and I don't want to surround myself with other people who have to live with it.'

'I'm sorry,' I signed, trying to ignore how disappointed I felt. 'I won't mention it again.' I offered her my hand and she took it before we began walking.

'Thank you.' There were a few moments of silence before she began to speak in a whisper. 'I'm just not ready to think about my future yet. I've had so many options taken away from me, that I can't help but feel pissed off when I think about it. I really am sorry, Emily.'

'It's okay.' I was glad that we'd avoided what could have been our first argument, but still felt unsatisfied knowing that Alana was happier to live in denial than to accept how her life had changed. I reasoned that at least she had all the time she needed to figure out her future. 'Shall we go to Vellichor?'

'We shall.'

We slipped into Vellichor unnoticed, whilst Mrs Wilson served customers and Mr Costas cleared tables, and we crept through to the far end of the shop. There was a children's section, with beanbags and cushions covering the floor, and we sat together beside the Wendy house reading nook.

'So... girlfriend,' I signed. 'I've never had a girlfriend before.'

'Neither have I.' Alana started to pick up the books that had been scattered near her seat. She placed them on the small bookshelf, in what appeared to be colour order. I watched her, before passing her the abandoned books I could see. 'But now I've got one and I'm going to miss her when she leaves.' She slotted in a final picture book and I felt my body begin to slump.

'Is this about university?' I signed, when she looked back at me. Alana nodded. Without thinking, I continued. 'I could always live at home instead of moving away.'

Alana pursed her lips. 'You can't do that, Emily.'

'But I think that's what I want; I want to stay with you.' Truthfully, I wasn't entirely sure what I wanted:

on the one hand, I did want to stay at home, with Alana and my parents. On the other hand, moving away for university had always been my plan. I hated having to choose. 'I think so, anyway. I love you.'

Alana started to wring her hands, the side of her foot brushing repeatedly against the jigsaw-style rug. 'Emily, you can't just change your plans because you love me; you don't know if you want to stay here.'

'Do you not want me to?' I signed, regretting it as soon as I did so. I realised I was inadvertently guilt-tripping her, but Alana replied before I could apologise.

'Of course I want you to! I hate the thought of looking into your room and not seeing you standing there. That doesn't mean you should give up your uni experience though.'

'But I'm really going to miss you.'

'And I'll miss you too, but every great love story has some struggle, right?' As I nodded, Alana jumped up and weaved through the shelves over to the classics section. She returned a few seconds later with a copy of *Great Expectations*, and I thought back to the first time we'd met. To the book that had shown us we had things in common. As she sat back down, she flicked open the front cover. 'I mean, Pip ends up with Estella against all odds.'

'He does,' I signed. Judging by the smile on Alana's face, she'd found an inscription. 'Is there anything written there?'

'Your story is worth more than you think. Make sure that you're alive to tell it,' she read aloud.

'I like that quote.'

'Me too.' Alana closed the book again. 'Though, if your story and my story are both worth a lot, how much is *our* story worth?'

'At least as much as Pip and Estella's,' I answered with a smile. Alana laughed and turned the book over, pointing at the list of recommended book titles.

'More than Daisy and Gatsby's?'

God, I loved her. 'Definitely.'

'Well maybe one day we'll inspire our own book. Emily and Alana can be the next literary OTP.'

There was absolutely nothing that I wanted more; I wanted our love to be preserved forever. Though, of course, my next words and signs came out cynically before I could stop them.

'As amazing as we are, Al, I'm not so sure I can imagine that.'

'I can,' she said. 'Years from now, some great poet will describe a pale girl with wild orange hair and a short girl with eyes like stars and they'll say...' Her gaze drifted back to the book in her hand. 'They'll say that the two of them loved with a love that was more than love.' She recited her musings in a falsely dramatic tone, clutching her other hand to her heart, and I couldn't help but laugh.

'Isn't that –?'

'Edgar Allan Poe,' we said in unison.

'You know, they never discovered what he died of,' I signed, thinking back to my GCSE English classes. Our teacher had made us write author fact files for every novel we studied, including *The Raven*. 'How sad is that?'

'That is really sad,' Alana agreed after a pause. 'Even sadder than the fact that I was going to kiss you then, until you brought up the subject of death.'

'Oh. Well, you could kiss me anyway.' I felt a flush of pride; that was genuinely quite smooth for me. Alana seemed to be thinking the same; she leaned forward, her eyes closed and her lips slightly parted. I leaned forward too, but I just couldn't help myself. I spoke into her ear, unsure if I wanted her to be able to hear or not. 'They think it could have been a brain tumour.'

Chapter 15

'You're back early!' said my dad as we walked in that afternoon. He was ironing one of his work suits in the living room. 'Is Alana joining us for game night later?'

I translated his words for Alana, who was standing at the bottom of the stairs.

'Do you think Mum will be okay with that?' I asked, only half-joking.

Alana smiled, before she quickly signed 'don't worry about me'. As if that was a possibility.

'Of course she'll be okay; Alana's practically family now.'

'You're basically family,' I signed to Alana. I raised my eyebrows, almost daring her to challenge the statement. 'Thanks, Dad!' I added, before we ran upstairs.

Alana called out her own 'thank you' as we did so, and I wondered if she ever would be part of my family one day, or if it was far too soon to even think about marrying her. It was strange; I'd never once pictured myself having a life with James outside of being eighteen. Never. But Alana? I could see us having the time of our lives together, up until we were old and grey.

'You finished it?' I heard Alana's voice coming from inside my bedroom, and I realised I'd been too distracted to follow her inside. I walked in and saw her standing beside the painted canvases I'd propped up against the wall. Alana's sea picture was hidden behind my portrait of her.

'Nearly, but there's something missing. I don't know what.' I looked at the painting again as if I'd suddenly be able to figure it out.

'I think it's amazing as it is. I almost feel like Dorian Gray.'

'Alana! He is not a character you want to embody.'

She giggled. 'And you've made me look really pretty.'

No matter how many times she did it, I still felt my heart soar every time Alana complimented my artwork.

'That wasn't hard; you are pretty.' And strong, and brave, and kind, and perfect. For once, I was glad that I wasn't completely fluent in BSL yet; in that moment, I wouldn't have been able to stop myself from describing how incredible Alana was.

'Wow, you're so gay,' said Alana, sitting down on my bed. 'So, so gay.'

'Nope; I'm definitely bisexual.' I pulled out the ocean canvas and hid it behind my legs. Alana tried to peer behind me. 'But, speaking of how in love with you I am –' I cringed at the fact that I'd said that aloud. More importantly, at the fact that I'd signed it. 'I painted something for you.'

'For me?'

I reached behind me and picked up the canvas before handing it to her. She looked down at it, her lips slightly parted, and her eyes crinkled.

'Emily.'

'I know that looking at waves isn't the same as hearing them, but I wanted to paint your favourite sound for you, so it can help you remember it.'

Her voice was thick, as if she was holding back tears. 'Thank you, it's beautiful.'

I felt myself beginning to shake; I hadn't meant to make her cry. 'Alana, I'm so sorry. I didn't mean to upset you! If you don't want it, I –'

'It's not that,' she interrupted, though my hand gestures were so wild that I was amazed she'd understood me. 'Honestly, it's perfect.' She cleared her throat. 'I should say, though, water stopped being my favourite sound quite soon after I met you.'

I hoped against hope that she was joking; I didn't want to believe I'd spent hours perfecting a picture of the sea only for her to prefer something else. I wondered if maybe I'd found myself getting distracted around her, just like I'd always done with James; maybe she'd told me her new favourite sound and I just hadn't listened to her as well as I'd thought I had.

'So, what's your favourite sound now?'

'It's you.' She didn't give me a chance to reply or protest, though I could feel myself relaxing. 'Your voice and your laugh are the sounds that I miss hearing properly. I'd give anything to have known you longer so I could have heard them more.'

In that moment, I had no idea what to say; not only was that the nicest thing anybody had ever said to me, but it was also the saddest. I sat down beside her.

'I'm not painting you a picture of me,' I said eventually.

Alana pouted and batted her eyes. 'But why? This one's beautiful, and I thank you for it, but you're better than waves any day.'

'You don't need a painting of me, because you're never losing me. You'll see my face every day until it's all…' I started to fingerspell. 'Wrinkly and gross, I promise.'

Alana laughed. 'If only I'd gone blind instead of deaf, then I wouldn't mind.' I opened my mouth in pretend shock, but she continued before I could reply. 'I have something for you too.'

'You do?'

'On the day we picked up my hearing aids, do you remember me telling you about sign names?'

I nodded slowly; of course I remembered. I never wanted to forget a minute I had spent with her. 'Yeah, I remember.'

'I thought of one for you,' she said, before signing silently. I felt my breath catch in my throat.

'Is that?'

'Yes. It's very fitting, if I do say so myself.'

We stayed in my room for over an hour. Between kisses, we talked and signed about date ideas for the summer, and we ensured that we were always making physical contact with each other. Then, when my mum got home, she came into my room to personally invite Alana to game night. A few minutes later, we joined her and my dad downstairs.

If She Favours You

'Finally, you're here!' he exclaimed. He was filling plastic bowls with different flavours of crisps and popcorn.

'Thanks for having me,' Alana replied.

My mum nodded and signed 'you're welcome', as my dad left to retrieve more food.

'So, what game were you thinking we could play?' I asked my mum, signing as I did so to ensure that Alana could follow the conversation.

'Your dad wanted Battleship, but I was thinking charades.'

'Because Battleship is the champion of all games!' my dad called from the kitchen.

My mum clicked her tongue, almost as if she'd already had that conversation, and picked up a wicker box from the floor. Around Christmas time last year (AKA when we'd last listened to my mum's game suggestion), we had filled it with folded pieces of paper, all showing a title of a film or a book. I turned to Alana to fill her in on what was happening.

'My mum wants to play C-H-A-R-A-D-E-S.'

Alana raised her eyebrows as she silently copied my fingerspelling. It only took me a few seconds to realise why she looked so bewildered at the prospect of playing that game.

'She won't even have thought.' I glanced at my mum. 'I'm so sorry.'

'No, don't be sorry,' Alana signed, just as my dad walked back in. 'Don't say anything. You do the acting.' She slowed down her actions as my dad joined my mum on their end of the couch. Neither of them were watching us. 'And you can just do the actual sign for whatever the word is.'

I shook my head in disbelief, but my smile gave away the fact that I was secretly impressed. Family game night was about to become a lot more interesting.

'Me and Mark will be team one,' said my mum. 'And you girls can be together.'

'That's perfect, Mrs Davis.'

'Please Alana, it's Sarah,' Mum signed in response. I held my breath, wondering if she was going to realise that she'd just challenged a hard of hearing girl to a game of charades. Fortunately, she didn't.

'Stop sucking up to her!' I signed to Alana. She kissed me in response, before pulling away with a huge grin on her face.

'Okay, Mark, who should do the acting first?'

My dad had just filled his hands with popcorn. 'Ladies first, always.'

'Right.' Mum pulled a piece of paper out of the box and nodded at it. She walked into the middle of the room, then pretended to open a book.

'It's a book!' Dad said, his mouth full of popcorn. I reached for some myself as my mum nodded and held up three fingers. 'A book title with three words.' Mum held up two fingers before beginning to rub her stomach with her hands, a pained expression on her face. 'Pregnant?' She shook her head. 'Belly? Stomach? Baby? Tummy?'

After each of my dad's guesses, my mum's hands quickened their pace and her eyes became wider. Eventually, she went back to holding up three fingers.

'Did he get it right?' I asked, fairly certain that none of my dad's suggestions had been plausible. My mum shook her head, still holding up three fingers. She then pointed at the board game shelf on the far wall.

'Shelf? There? Across? Wall?' My mum stomped over to it and held up two of the games. 'Games! Is it games?' She nodded and put them back before standing in front of us again. She rubbed her forehead.

'We are so going to win this.' Alana whispered in my ear. I had to agree.

My mum held up two fingers again.

'Back to the second word!' My dad's enthusiasm hadn't wavered anywhere near as much as hers had. She went back to rubbing her stomach, her face creased up in pain that I wasn't entirely sure she was faking. 'Labour? Cramps? Contractions!' My mum groaned as she looked round the room, her eyes finally landing on the popcorn. Still with one hand on her stomach, she pointed at the food. 'Food? Hungry? Hunger! The Hunger Games!'

'Finally!' My mum flung her arms out to the side. 'That should not have taken so long.'

'It was rather excruciating,' I said.

'We'll still beat you, I'm sure.' My mum returned to her seat.

'But we won't even need to use props.' I waggled my eyebrows at her and jumped up, ready to sign. I took a piece of paper out of the box as my mum nudged my dad.

'Why did you automatically assume it was pregnancy?'

'No, I just –' He stopped himself when my mum laughed, and he held her hand in his. 'It's Emily and Alana's turn now, acushla.'

I watched my mum rest her head on his shoulder and trace a shape on the back of his hand. He leaned into her. I turned my attention to Alana and pretended to draw a rectangle in front of myself, using my forefingers. I then pretended to read a book.

'A TV show and a book?' she said. I nodded, before holding up two fingers. 'With two words.' I nodded again and put my fingers down before holding them both up again. 'Second word.' I made my hand into a fist and brought it up to my chin, before moving it down as if to symbolise a beard. Alana narrowed her eyes slightly. 'Man?'

I rubbed my thumb and forefinger together to sign 'almost.'

'Men? Mr Men!'

'Perfect!' I exclaimed, signing it too. I high fived Alana as I sat back down beside her. My parents were watching us, their mouths slightly open.

'How on earth –?' my mum began.

'Are you a bit jealous?' I signed as I spoke, Alana chuckling beside me. I watched as the realisation dawned on them.

'That's cheating! You can't use sign language in charades! You two are ruining the good name of family game night.' My dad was shaking his head, no longer curled up with my mum, but his eyes were crinkled, as if he was trying not to laugh.

'Sorry Mr and Mrs Davis, but I've never heard that rule.' Alana signed as she spoke too, my mum watching her intently.

'Oh my goodness. I can't believe I suggested charades and I didn't even think about you,' she said, her cheeks tinged pink. 'I'm sorry Alana,' she signed.

'Mrs Davis, it's fine, honestly! I enjoyed playing.'

'I didn't enjoy losing though.' My dad heaved himself off the couch before picking up one of the board game boxes. 'And so, we challenge you two to Battleship.'

'Game on,' said Alana, before winking at me.

We both got off the couch, joining my parents on the floor around the table. We sat opposite them, the board between us, and set up our side of the game.

As Alana put her arm around my waist, drawing me in closer, I let my eyes close for a few moments. I could feel myself smiling as I considered how my life had changed over the course of one less-than-predictable summer. I let out a little laugh. After my dad announced that him and my mum were ready, I opened my eyes again. Alana was looking at me, her lips curled upwards.

'You okay?' she whispered.

I kissed her.

Author's Note

I want to start this off by saying thank you to everyone who has read this novel. I spent four years daydreaming about these characters and their story, and am beyond thrilled that others can now share them with me. My aim was to write a short book that read as easily as fanfiction, and I do hope I succeeded.

As a lesbian author, I know how important representation is in the media, and I want to do my very best to help people who feel invisible get their experiences 'out there'. With that being said, I have a number of other people I'd like to thank for helping me get *If She Favours You* out into the world.

In order to accurately portray Alana's life as a hard of hearing person, I reached out to multiple members of the Deaf community. Each one of them opened my eyes to a new way of living, and I'd like to thank them all for helping me see beyond my own experience of the world.

I'm also very grateful to my university tutors and secondary school English teacher, for they collectively taught me more about writing than I could have hoped for.

My family, who I mentioned at the very start, deserve my gratitude for providing me with unconditional love and support my whole life. My dog, who has slept on me dutifully through countless drafts, too deserves a huge thank you.

I'd also like to thank my partner, who shows me the kind of love one thinks only exists in books.

About the Author

Harley Rose lives in the UK with her dog, her family, and a huge mountain of unused notebooks.

She can be found on Twitter (@HarleyRoseYA) and Tumblr (@ifshefavoursyou).

As well as novels, she enjoys writing poetry, short stories, and lengthy paragraphs complimenting Taylor Swift on her newest songs.

www.ingramcontent.com/pod-product-compliance
Lightning Source LLC
LaVergne TN
LVHW091543060526
838200LV00036B/691